THE RETURN OF
HUNTER S.
THOMPSON
AN UNTOLD STORY OF NAZI HUNTING

VOLUME 2

J. MICHAEL MORIARTY

THE RETURN OF HUNTER S. THOMPSON
VOLUME 2
Copyright © 2021 J. Michael Moriarty

Printed in the United States of America

ISBN: 978-1-09837-395-5
ISBN eBook: 978-1-09837-396-2

DEDICATION

This series is dedicated to brother Tom. Oldest of the Moriarty boys. He left us at the end of the most difficult year 2020.

He is still with us in spirit; I am starting to understand and realize. In spirit. What that means. A learning experience to be sure. Anyway, Tom understands what I'm trying to say.

Hunter was one of those guys we cheered on as the rebel and iconoclast. He was not afraid to rock the boat: the System.

Maybe he went too far, but that happens. He tried to be a reporter who feared nothing and nobody. He succeeded in that effort.

Tom and I give him a chance at redemption, not that he needs it.

We plug Hunter into the world of hunting Nazis. He is young and has the energy needed for this massive endeavor.

Tom and I know one thing. Hunter Thompson would have been a great Nazi hunter. In fact, he is. Check it out. Read on.

ACKNOWLEDGEMENTS

I started my writing journey four years ago today. It was a few short weeks after the passing of the legendary Irish writer Frank Delaney, who I am honored to have known.

My brother Tom and I met Frank at a book reading at the Kansas City Library.

"We just missed you by a few days at your book reading in Tipperary," Tom said.

"What were you doing in Ireland?" Frank asked.

"Just visiting friends in County Tipperary at the white house on the hill across from Thomastown Castle."

"I grew up in Thomastown and my main character Charles O'Brien in the book *Tipperary* lives in that house on the hill, Mick." After feeling an amazing sense of coincidence, we continued talking and Frank told us what it was like doing his book reading in Tipperary town.

I'll never forget world traveler Frank Delaney said he was nervous returning home to do a book reading from the book *Tipperary*.

But his fears were laid to rest when the town's folk started to ask about different people and places in the book.

"It was great. Sorry you Moriarty boys missed it."

Well, I remember Frank's words and his advice about doing book readings. As I now prepare to do book readings of my own recent writings, I also reflect on advice from Frank's beloved wife Diane Meier. I thank them both. Thank you, Frank. Thank you, Diane.

J. Michael (Mick) Moriarty
March 17, 2021

INTRODUCTION

This is the second book in a series about Hunter S. Thompson as a Nazi hunter in 1958. He is 21 years old, out of the Air Force and following through on a commitment he made with his friend Jordan to hunt down Nazis when they grew up.

They have taken some time off from a period of sustained Nazi chasing and they have been told by their mentor that they need to review and do write-ups on their activities to date. These will be used for training of future Nazi hunters.

The mentor for Hunter and Jordan is Tom Charlebois, formerly French Resistance, World War II. Tom is the manager of a hotel in London, El Duque, the Duke Hotel.

During this period of recording and refreshing recollections, Hunter suggests visiting the oldest pubs in the city.

CONTENTS

CHAPTER 1

HUNTER AND HOLMES

TOM WAS VERY CLEAR ABOUT wanting us to take a break from chasing down Nazis. We were in London and Tom insisted we stay close-by, just in case. Also, he was concerned for our safety and thought we would be better off staying in London rather than going anywhere else. He was right, of course. Tom was always right.

We spent weeks, nearly an entire month, going to museums during the day and to the theater in the evenings.

Sometime I'll write down a few notes about those great and interesting times. For now, I should probably disclose what happened after that month of pulling back from the Nazi hunting.

Hunter proposed we visit the oldest pubs in the city. "We'll learn as much there as we will at the museums," Hunter promised.

The journey was fun. The Guinea, The Spaniards Inn, Hoop & Grapes, Lamb & Flag, Cittie of Yorke, The Old Bell, Ye Olde Cheshire Cheese, Ye Olde Mitre, The Prospect of Whitby, The Seven Stars. There were a few more, and all of them produced enough stories for Hunter to write a 300 page anthology of short stories. But not now.

There was also a pub we visited called the Northumberland Arms at Charing Cross in the center of London. The visit was Hunter's idea. He said there was a museum exhibit at the pub which made no sense until we got there.

It turned out this pub had an exhibit created for the 1951 Festival of Britain. It was the contents of the Sherlock Holmes and Dr. Watson flat. Everything at 221 B Baker Street was in a room above the pub. We were told it was so authentic that you could feel the presence of Holmes and Watson.

"Can I help you gentlemen?" a man inquired. "This will soon be called the Sherlock Holmes Public House. We are having a name change as a result of the Holmes exhibit getting a permanent home here."

"That's great," Hunter said. "We are very happy for you. It is all so life-like and so real."

"Right. Yes, very right," the man said as he sort of stumbled through his brief affirmation.

"What is the commotion about?" another man inquired.

"We were just commenting on the great recreation of 221 B Baker Street," I said.

"Yes, John and I are both happy at how it all worked out. It gives us a chance to get back in the game."

"What game is that, sir?" Hunter asked.

"Just the game of life, really. Nothing more. A chance for redemption, you know. We never really finished our tasks that we set out for ourselves. It all ended too soon, but now we have a chance to make up for lost time and unfulfilled promises."

"Promises for what?" Hunter asked.

"To eradicate evil, of course," he said.

"And redemption for what?" Hunter asked.

"Just, you know, we never finished the job. We never finished, did we?"

"No, John. We never did."

"Are you guys like vigilantes or something?" I inquired.

"Are we sir? I've never thought we were."

"No, John, of course not," the articulate one said. "Vigilantism is outside the law. We have always worked within the law. Sometimes ahead of law enforcement, but always mindful of the law. Vigilantes resort to mob violence oftentimes. We stand foursquare against that world."

"Follow me this way so we can sit down and talk," the tall man said.

So we did. We walked to the side of the room where there was a door and above it was the address famous to all Sherlock Holmes fans: 221 B Baker Street.

Everything changed on the other side of the door. The room was spacious and it was an ultimate Sherlock Holmes room. There was a massive library, several large chairs, a selection of violins and a rack with at least 20 pipes. There was a large fireplace with a mantle stacked with open books. There was also an area of the room which contained several scientific instruments useful for measurement and analysis. And there were no fewer than a dozen magnifying glasses and several microscopes.

"I'm starting to think this is almost real," I said.

"You are right, indeed. Dr. Watson and I are back. And we intend to help you. We know about terrible crimes committed by the criminal empire that was the Third Reich. Any assistance you need from us, we are more than ready to help."

"That is very generous of you to offer your services. We will let you know of any upcoming assignments here in England," I said.

"As you know from your studies, we have done most of our work in London. The rest is around England. It is rare for us to leave England, but if necessary, for a mission, we will travel."

"There is one footnote to this limitation on travel," Watson said.

"Of course," Holmes affirmed.

"During the 'Great Hiatus' when Holmes was gone for three years he did travel to Persia, Tibet, Sudan (Khartoum) and finally France."

"It's generally believed I was working for the Crown during that period. I really can't affirm or deny. You understand I am sure.

"But mainly I prefer working on the home turf. I seem to do better work close to home."

"Thank you," Hunter said. "We will stay in touch."

"Let us know and tell Tom hello," they said together.

"Of course."

As we left the private chambers of Mr. Holmes, we discussed what had just taken place. We met Sherlock Holmes and Dr. John Watson. Nothing would ever be the same again.

We called Tom to request meeting soon. He was in France visiting family so next day we decided to make a return visit to see Sherlock Holmes instead. We had a lot of questions. The first one, was this a hoax?

"Good morning boys," he said. "I expected you earlier, really. You probably think this could be a hoax. Of course, my assumption is based on knowing Tom is out of town, so you have no exact way of confirming my statements to you. Further, you have learned that in this business of tracking and hunting criminals there is no substitute for hard proof. Verifiable evidence. Clearly you are developing and using the skills of trackers. That's what we are, trackers. We track criminals. Nazis are ultimately criminals. They blame their actions on the war, but the war did not make them rob their victims and commit genocide against an entire race."

"I'm sorry to have questioned your identity and your veracity, sir," I said. "I have no doubt now."

"I agree," Hunter said. "We are nevertheless a little surprised of our chance meeting, if that's what it was… but it probably wasn't. Was it?" Hunter asked.

"No, not at all," the great detective said. "I am allowed to come back during periods when the powers that be determine my help is essential. That's what we have here. These Nazis escaped in droves after the war crimes and they stole the wealth of people of several nations.

"I was involved in the war effort of the Great War and World War II. Those were both special appearances given to me posthumously by the soul of Sir Arthur Conan Doyle. I can't explain how or why. That, of course, flies in the face of our discussion on proof, scientific proof. However, I only add that my mentor was most concerned that I always be available when I was needed. In other words, there will always be wars and crises. Ever since that fateful day at the Reichenbach Falls in Switzerland it has been like that. Sometimes, my reemergence is noted or obvious, and other times not. We shall see what happens here. For the time being only a few people are aware of my return. Of course, I also mean to include my associate and forever assistant and personal biographer, John Watson."

"I was starting to wonder if you remembered I was still here," Watson said.

We all laughed. He did too. He wasn't at all what I expected. Watson looked as rugged as a sailor and as tough as a pirate, whereas Holmes was exactly the Holmes one would expect. Tall, swift, precocious, confident and charming in a non-offensive way. There could only be one person like this, Mr. Sherlock Holmes.

As we returned to his study we were invited to sit down. Although tea was offered, we decided on water which we promptly splashed on our faces.

"It's just so hard to believe," Hunter said. "I spent much of my childhood following you in the pages of several books and dozens of short stories. My brain is having trouble computing."

"Just let it go," Holmes said. "I have the same problem. I can't believe I'm here and this is me. But I just do what needs to be done and move on. There is too much work to do. We don't have time to bring in Freud.

"Do we John?"

"Certainly not, Sherlock," Watson said. "That was long ago and worth forgetting. We don't need Sigmund to figure out the Nazis. We can handle that. We need the help of the Almighty in this mission."

"And I would add we also need some good information from some people on the inside," Holmes said. "I suggest a visit to one of our friends at Bletchley Park."

"We worked on our first project with Bletchley people," Hunter said.

"Right, you did," Holmes said.

"Oh, you know," I said.

"I think we started that ball rolling," Watson said.

"Sorry, sir," Hunter said.

"Not a problem. How could you have known?"

"Exactly," Hunter said.

"With just one exception," Sherlock said.

"Yes, one exception," Watson added.

"Mr. Horwithy did have you meet with his boss, Professor Semloh," Holmes said.

"I get it. Like an anagram or palindrome," I said.

"More like a semordnilap," Holmes said. "The word in reverse is not the same, but different. H-O-L-M-E-S and S-E-M-L-O-H."

"The palindrome would be like civic and level," Watson said. "And the anagram would be some other configuration of letters for H-O-L-M-E-S like E-S-H-O-L-M as a name."

"Enough word play. That was me, Professor Semloh, briefing you on the diabolical Ravenmaster."

"Yes, of course," Hunter said. "You have always loved your disguises. As boys, my brother and I would often dress up in costumes whish were based on your disguises.

"I was often the sailor while my brother was the minister. Or, I was the old book collector and my brother was the drunken groom.

"I still remember for my tenth birthday that my brother bought me a book called the *Disguises of Sherlock Holmes: An Illustrated Analysis of Thirty Disguises*. That was our bible.

"Anyway, I can't say we are surprised at the deception. It was straight out of your playbook, sir," Hunter said.

"Yes, yes. I think we should drop the 'sir' if we're going to be working together, Hunter."

"We will try to drop the 'sir' but it may not be easy."

"It's okay to call me Doctor," Watson said. "He calls me John, as you may have noticed."

"So, what should we do at Bletchley and whom to see?" Hunter asked.

"Believe it or not you will see another Horwithy. No joke this time. You need to see Faith Horwithy. She will update you boys on current information and intelligence on all Nazi operations which are continuing without interruption. Once you get up to speed, we will be available to provide any insight and assistance we can."

We were provided a ride to Bletchley Park although we offered to take the train. "There isn't time to waste so do take the ride," Holmes said. "We need to keep you moving. Like right away."

"Sure, sure," Hunter said. "I'm starting to get pretty good using the trains here, but you're calling the shots Mr. Holmes."

"Thank you. Now, Watson, please have Mr. K get these boys out to Bletchley Park."

"Right away, Holmes."

"Who is Mr. K?" I asked.

"He is Reginald Krakowski, a cousin of Jerzy Rozycki and a student of Henryk Zygalski. They were part of the Polish team of mathematicians who helped England crack the Enigma Code early in 1939. The Enigma machine was used by the Germans to send messages by code. The other member of the Polish code breakers was Marian Rejewski. These three Poles have a special place at Bletchley Park."

Upon arriving at Bletchley Park (BP, as we called it), Mr. Krakowski took us to the site of the future memorial for the Polish mathematicians.

"And they weren't the only ones trying to help England save the world from Hitler," Krakowski said. "The famous Polish pilots of the 303 Squadron also came to this country to help fight. They were among the best pilots in the RAF during the Battle of Britain. They called England the last hope. Last Hope Island, they said."

We thanked Mr. K for telling us about the importance of the Polish assistance in the war against Hitler. He then took us directly to Faith Horwithy who was waiting for our arrival in a conference room in the main structure of the intelligence complex at Bletchley Park.

"Good day gentlemen," Faith Horwithy said. "I will dispense with the niceties and social graces because it is important that you get up to speed quickly."

"You have been briefed on prewar Nazi espionage in England. There were many Nazis here who tried to infiltrate our way of life. As you know, they were not successful in their efforts. Some were returned to Germany. Others were imprisoned in Britain. The problem is Nazis who came to this country after the war under false pretenses. There is a group of ex-Nazis living in London. Mr. Holmes is convinced they are up to no good, so we intend to do something about that. Specifically, we intend to have you, Hunter and Jordan, infiltrate this group of former guards from the Trawniki training camp."

"How?" Hunter asked.

"I wish we knew. That's the problem," Miss Horwithy said.

"I'm sure we can come up with some plans," I said. "I know about Trawniki and what they did there. I also know who was there. They weren't German Nazis. They were from Eastern Europe – from Romania, Lithuania, Hungary and Ukraine. They are all liars too. They got trained at Trawniki and then went to Treblinka, Sobibor or Belzec to work at the gas chambers. We know Poland had a population of over

3 million Jews before the Nazis invaded. In less than two years after the invasion of Poland, one-half of the Jews in the country were dead as a result of Operation Reinhard. Reinhard Heydrich was an SS general and Holocaust promoter."

"We will help you devise a plan," Faith Horwithy said.

"That's not all," Faith added. "They all were trained by the German SS and they even wore uniforms acting just like the Nazis. They claim they did no harm and that they were just clerical workers or kitchen labor. But we know better. We know many are the still missing, like Ivan the Terrible, the brutal guard from Trawniki and Treblinka. And our goal is to find them.

"It's all true and worse," Horwithy said. "I know you understand."

"You are right, Faith," Hunter said. "Jordan knows whereof he speaks. We will come up with a plan and coordinate with Mr. Holmes."

"That will be the best way to go," she said. "I'll go over these files with you and then you can get started on the mission."

And that's the way it went at Bletchley Park.

Soon we were back in the quarters of Holmes and Watson. By the time we got back there we had come up with a plan to get inside this group of former Trawniki trained guards, so we ran it by Mr. Holmes.

"Sounds like a great idea but I think it needs an additional person to make it work," Holmes said.

"I think Fabian and Philly Boudreau need to have one of their principals with them to make the deal,' he added.

"Maybe so," I said. "We can work on a strategy for the proposed art transactions."

"I think we do what Otto did in our last meeting," Hunter aid. "We give them a valuable work of art to show good faith. Then we hire them to be our guards for upcoming major transactions of an international nature. We offer art, money and some prestige. They'll do it."

"We can give them the painting Otto gave us," Hunter said. "The Two Riders on the Beach, by Max Lieberman. It's perfect. It even has Nazi provenance. From one Nazi to another."

"That is exceptionally devious Hunter," Mr. Holmes said.

"Thank you sir. I hope to be remembered for such deceptiveness when it comes to dealing with Nazis."

"Yes, they were terrible and did horrendous things," Holmes said. "The Trawniki trained guards were the labor force that made the German policy of Final Solution possible."

"I should tell you that Faith Horwithy and the Bletchley Park experts believe there is a conspiracy ongoing with the Trawniki guards. They believe the guards who are living all over England, admittedly under false pretenses, have congregated in London to carry out their plans to thwart and derail all investigations into their cover up of what they did during the war. Investigators in the United States and Europe have developed evidence on the Trawniki guards and it will become damaging as it is developed by the prosecutors and investigators. It is only a matter of time before these guards face their accusers and their justice.

"This is what we found," Holmes said. "They will make an all-out attempt to eliminate evidence. That means they will go after the witnesses which means they will resort to their training. They are killers. You boys are entering into a mission of certain violence. I have been through this kind of thing before. Tom knows my record. That's why I'm involved."

"I think we're ready to deal with these men," Hunter said.

"I agree," I said.

"Well, sorry to say, I don't think any of us is prepared to deal with the level of depravity that exists among the men of Trawniki," Holmes said. "These are the men who led prisoners off the trains, marched them into the forest and pushed them into large pits where they were shot. Thousands of people were killed in this brutal and terrifying way. Some of their victims were Jews from the town of Lublin, where there were 40,000 Jews before the war; after the war only a few hundred. The madness of this killing, which included women and children, is incomprehensible."

"My God, they are vicious and mad killers," Watson said. "You boys will need to do exactly what Holmes says. This is almost too dangerous for even you, Holmes."

"I agree, John, but we will have backup from the SAS (Special Air Service)."

"They are certainly the best special forces unit in England," Watson said. "Who dares wins."

"That's right Watson. That's their motto. They are known as The Regiment.

"In Africa during World War II Churchill wanted to create a commando unit of elite soldiers. That was the beginning. All of their missions were perilous, often doing sabotage behind enemy lines or in enemy controlled waters like the Bay of Biscay at Bordeaux where they mined German cargo vessels.

"We will be backed up by the SAS on the military aspects," Holmes said. "But we need to set up the whole ruse with the art business."

"Once we get our meeting with their lead guys, the Reimer brothers, we will propose hiring the group as our security force. We know they're armed and dangerous, and we know they need money."

"It seems like whenever there are guns and danger there are usually men from Mossad around," I said. "Will they be working with SAS on this project?"

"I'm sure they would like to be involved. I'll tell Tom about your idea. My guess is Tom has returned from France and already set a plan with Mossad. I will review plans with him. Also, Watson and I will contact our sources with The Regiment.

"We will meet with my contact Sgt Mac McAleese of SAS."

We left Holmes and Watson as we needed to get ourselves organized for our next Nazi encounter. We were glad to find out Tom had returned from France and would be able to meet with us later that day.

It was not long before he returned to his place downstairs at El Duque and met with us.

"I'm just back from France and it sounds like the next operation is in full swing. I left a meeting with some of my old friends at SAS. They are ready to help as necessary. But we also need Mossad assistance. I can explain."

Tom did explain that his plan was foolproof, contingent on only one thing; we needed to sell the art story to the Reimers so they would engage their group to travel with us as our security team.

CHAPTER 2

THE NAZI CHASE CONTINUES

WE TRAVELLED TO THE MUNICH Sports Club in London with the security (SAS) driver in a private car. We brought the bait with us, the Two Riders on the Beach painting by Max Lieberman. When we crossed Birdcage Walk our driver Jimmy said we were close to the Bavarian club. "Are you boys ready?" Jimmy asked. "Don't worry about those idiots. We have reinforcements in the area that can come in to help for any emergency."

Our first problem was the sign on the door of the German club said "Closed. Private engagement."

We politely knocked on the door and were told in person the place was closed.

"You don't understand," Hunter said. "We are guests making a surprise visit. Reimer will be upset if you don't let us in."

"Let me check that package or box you are carrying," the doorman said.

"That's a problem," Hunter said. "Maybe your English aint so good. This is the surprise as part of our surprise visit. Get it?"

"Sir, there's no reason to be rude."

"Yeah, and there aint no reason to be stupid either," Hunter blasted back. "Just get Reimer."

"What's the commotion about," the new man at the door asked.

"We are here to see Reimer, that's all."

"I'm Reimer. Come in. How can I help you, sir?"

"We need to talk privately," I said. "This concerns a matter of some urgency."

We entered a drawing room off the foyer and were met by a second man.

"I'm Frank Reimer. This is brother Helmuth. What do you need from us?"

"Our business associate in America told us—I'm Fabian and this is cousin Philly Boudreaux—that we could hire security help in London for our art business. So, basically, Otto Von Krupp, now Otto Brown, told us to contact the Reimers in London for security services."

"What kind of security services are you talking about?" Frank Reimer asked.

"For international art trade. Otto said you were reliable," I said.

"I'm not sure I know Otto," Helmuth said.

"Well you know the family. His brother Klaus Von Krupp was a pretty famous rocket scientist. A Munich man."

"Yes, yes, of course," Frank said.

"What is the surprise?"

"This is a down payment and a showing of good faith. It is a painting which comes directly from Otto Von Krupp, who is located in America. He said this painting would convince you to help us with security demands in the upcoming months as we develop our relationship with Otto's partners.

"Please don't ask who they are," I said. "If I did know I would not be allowed to tell you. That is the nature of this business. It is private. It is confidential. Basically, all transactions of sale or trade are secret. It has to be that way."

"This painting from Otto is beautiful. Please thank him from both of us," Frank Reimer said.

"I'm sure we can provide security for you. Travel is not a problem. We are between contracts for security services with financial firms, so we are able to assist," Helmuth spoke up..

"How many men do you need?" Frank asked. "We have a large pool to draw on."

"I will inquire with our contact who speaks directly to Otto. In a recent meeting in Florida where valuable art was present on a yacht Otto had a security group of at least twenty men. Some of these get togethers involve masterworks of very high value. Much of Otto's art is modern and much of ours is more traditional. Our principals are attempting to make multiple trades in a volume never seen before."

"I see," Frank Reimer said.

"That makes sense," brother Helmuth chimed in.

"Otto represents a syndicate that acquired art during the war when the prices were low because of the depression," I said. "Now they would like to trade the modern art for the classics. We represent several private investors from Europe, and our business is based in Switzerland, although you can probably tell from our accents that we're Cajun boys from Louisiana.

"We will soon know where this next event will be. We saw Otto's inventory at our last meeting in Florida. At the next get together we will be taking several valuable works packed as prize cargo on a new 707 jet which can cross the Atlantic Ocean without refueling."

"We will cross that ocean or any other ocean as long as my people are fairly compensated," Frank Reimer said.

"We will work that out with no problem. Otto has vouched for you and your men."

"His donation of the painting is probably worth six figures, so we are serious," Hunter said.

"We're not doubting your ability to fund this project," Helmuth said. "We just need to make sure we are doing right by our people. The Reimers always look out for their people."

"All of our agreements need to be approved by a selected representative for our client group. This year it is Count Felix von Kramm who approves all contracts. He is outside in the car."

"Sure, by all means, have him come in," Frank Reimer said.

We gave the high sign to Jimmy McAleese that it was okay to send Mr. Holmes in to close the deal.

"Reimer brothers," I said, "this is Felix Von Kramm of Europe."

"Yes, I am Von Kramm. My presence here tonight means you will work with us on security for our upcoming event."

"We look forward to this new business alliance with your group," Frank Reimer said.

"My job is to make sure your men are up to the task. We need to review training and weaponry. This is going to require heavy arms in place. We can discuss details as soon as the site selection is complete."

"Originally, it looked like New York State would provide the most convenient location, but there was a problem with the authorities in that state," Hunter said.

"Last November our New York secured site for art sales was raided by government agents because the organized crime families of America were all there for a meeting of the mob. You may have heard about it.

"So, we won't be going to Appalachian, New York ever again," Hunter said.

"Our security forces provided by New York Protection Inc. got greedy and invited the wrong group. We won't use their services again. This is why we took Otto's recommendation to find a more private security group," Count Felix explained.

"Now, we are trying to get clearance to meet in more business-friendly Bermuda," Count Felix said.

"It is an honor to meet you, sir, Count Von Kramm," the brothers Reimers said in unison.

"Call me Felix. I used to be a Count, but now I'm not. I now live in Switzerland for privacy and tax reasons."

"We understand. All these governments want too much information. Even in our small security business the governments want to know too much that is private," Frank Reimer said. "Who do they think they are? Maybe we should move to Switzerland too."

"Good idea," Hunter said. "What are you waiting for? It is the best place for privacy with your funds and your business."

"I think we have an agreement men. I will be provided with the event schedule soon and then get the necessary info to your group. We'll talk soon. It looks like we are one week out, so do any training you need to do. I'm sure you have all the necessary weapons you need. We will load all weapons on the jet in protected cargo containers on the plane behind the seats. They will not be put in the lower hold of the airliner. If being trapped in the baggage compartment of a plane is bad for people, then it can't be good for guns," Count Von Kramm said.

"We agree," the Reimers said, again in unison. "It is refreshing to meet a business person who appreciates the value of high-quality care for weapons," Helmuth Reimer said.

Of course, we didn't tell the Reimers that SAS troops would be located behind their weapons. They would believe the back of the plane was full of prized art, not British commandos.

We left the Munich Sports Club with our plan set in action. Now we hoped it would be just a matter of time before the Trawniki Conspiracy would meet its fate.

As we rode back to our current sleeping quarters at the Mayfair Hotel (a respectable venue for art dealers), Hunter was clearly bothered by something Holmes said to the Reimers.

"I was racking my brain and then I realized the Count was really the King of Bohemia who attempted to pull the wool over your eyes," Hunter said.

"Very good, Hunter," Holmes said.

"You remember a *Scandal in Bohemia*," Holmes said. "I always liked the character in that disguise, Count Felix. I always thought he deserved another shot with the disguise."

"The big difference this time is I think the disguise and acting were believable," Hunter said.

"I think you are right. The Reimers took the bait and they are all in," Holmes said. "What was that New York organized crime business?"

"Last year it was a scandal in America, not Bohemia. I just took it to the house, as they say," Hunter said.

"He does that a lot," I said. "He wings it. Hunter is the ultimate wingman."

"I admire that trait," Holmes said. "It is an essential survival technique."

"Yes, and it works well meeting girls," I said.

"Is that so?" Holmes asked.

"Not always," Hunter said. "Irene Adler got away."

"Touché," Holmes said.

"I admired her," Holmes said. "That is true. She outsmarted me and saw through my disguise as a clergyman back then, but you need to remember, boys, she got married the day I met her. Despite what the Sherlock Holmes readers may think, there was no logical reason to fall in love with a married woman."

"Yes, of course," we replied.

"Especially not on the first day of marriage," Holmes said.

We all laughed together. Holmes did have a sense of humor.

Going to Bermuda

Count Felix did the job. The Reimers made contact with us the next day. They thanked us for the great and valuable painting. Also, they said Count Felix sealed the deal. After they met the great Count, the Reimers were sold on this new business arrangement. Further, they would be doing firearms training that afternoon and every day until the art event.

"Tell them we're going to Bermuda, Jordan," Mr. Holmes said. "Both SAS and Mossad agree it is the best place for this showdown. For me, Bermuda has a special meaning. In a way it is the source of inspiration that created me, the character Sherlock Holmes. I was modeled after Dr. Joseph Bell who once made a diagnosis of a patient who was in the British military in Bermuda without examination."

"What about exact times and details?"

"We leave one week from tomorrow, next Sunday, from Gatwick Airport. We can load all the gear on Saturday. We've arranged for truck transport of all equipment, i.e. weapons."

And so it went. That week we planned and planned, but it was really going to be in the hands of military men once the plane landed in Bermuda. SAS and Mossad. I would not want to be a member of the Trawniki Conspiracy.

"The flight to Bermuda will be one of luxury," Holmes said.

"When leaving Bermuda the Trawniki men will be in an Israeli military transport which is designed to transport prisoners. They will literally be in chains."

Then it was off to Bermuda with our newly hired security force. Tom said Holmes would stay behind in London. Why not. We rode along like we were babysitting federal prisoners in transport. We even had a private area on the plane to review "art" business. The Reimers managed their bunch. Food was provided in flight, but we told the Reimers they would be engaged in business upon landing so there would be no booze served on the plane.

Hunter went to visit the bunch during flight. He noticed several of the men drinking from personal flasks. *If they knew where their final destination really was they would all wish they had flasks full of booze or maybe a cyanide-laced concoction.*

We landed at Bermuda International Airport and two school buses came out to meet the plane. One bus was for the men and the other was for their guns, they were told.

The Mossad agents were dressed in gray jumpsuits like baggage handlers. They entered the rear of the plane and within seconds the SAS troops came out of the front and back of the plane with weapons drawn as they rushed the Trawniki men waiting to get on their bus. All the men were placed face down on the tarmac.

While being searched for weapons several handguns carried on person by our passengers were found. It didn't matter. SAS was prepared.

They ran the show at first since it was their jurisdiction. Within ten minutes an Israeli cargo plane moved into position and parked nearby. A cargo loading ramp was rolled out from the back underside of the plane. The prisoners were taken one at a time and secured in the POW transport plane.

There was a fair amount of swearing during the loading of prisoners. We knew that it would be loud and uncivil. It was.

It was over fast and the plane left for Ramat David Air Base in Northern Israel. From that secure facility it would only be a matter of time before these men of Trawniki were put on trial. Some would provide valuable information on the whereabouts and crimes of Nazi leaders. We were hopeful we would receive information that we could use on our future missions.

For the time being, we would return to London where work was being done by Holmes and Watson on the next effort.

It was discussed briefly prior to our departure to Bermuda but all we knew was that it would be very sensitive as the British government was involved.

CHAPTER 3

BAHAMA MAMA NAZI

"Boys, I have been in discussions with my brother who works for the Crown. When he gets in a bind, I am the one he comes to. You know from your readings about my career that Mycroft calls on me from time to time," Holmes said.

"This is good Sherlock," Watson said. "Being up front, you know, about Mycroft. I think we had worked together for years before I even knew there was a brother. Then, he was just a junior government official. Finally, when the submarine papers went missing and the young clerk Cadogan was found dead on the underground tracks, I learned Mycroft was a major figure in the government."

"Yes, Watson, I have learned to be more open, more transparent. I appreciate your polite scolding."

"We don't want to cause any friction, gentlemen," I said.

"Not a problem," Watson said.

"This is how we converse," Holmes said. "We have matured and there is a lot of personal history which is known to the world, so we have to respect that fact."

"Have you been meeting Mycroft at the Diogenes Club?" Hunter asked.

"Very astute, Hunter," Holmes said.

"Yes, we have been reviewing documents and the Government's file at the Diogenes Club."

"The Government has recently learned that it unwittingly gave some Nazis permission to travel to the Bahamas at the end of the war."

"This all goes back to Churchill," Watson said. "It was his idea to send Edward, Duke of Windsor, to the Bahamas as Governor in 1940."

"That is right Watson," Holmes said. "Churchill wanted him out of Europe as the war was starting to spread. Even though he had sympathy for the German Nazis, Edward was unaware that he was a target for a Nazi kidnapping scheme at that time."

"So, what's the problem in the Bahamas?" Hunter asked. "The Duke and his would-be queen Wallis Simpson left the Bahamas in 1945 at the end of the war. I think they moved back to Paris where they were married in 1937 after he abdicated from being King Edward VIII of Great Britain."

"All true, Hunter," Holmes said. "We believe that Nazis used that private residence in the Bahamas as a staging platform to get out of Germany and get to South America. Specifically, to Argentina.

"There is no evidence to show the Duke of Windsor enabled this Nazi escape conspiracy, but the Nazis took advantage of the former king's supposed divided loyalties. We all know he befriended Hitler and endorsed some of the Nazi propaganda points. Same with Simpson. She bought into the Nazi policies."

"Eventually, they must have seen what Hitler did was a moral catastrophe," I said. "But I can never get that picture out of my head where Hitler meets them and kisses her hand at his mountain retreat, the Berghof."

"During the war the Governor Duke would entertain in the Bahamas. He and his wife were international socialite people. Of course, visitors from around the world would come to the Bahamas to escape the cold. Also, to escape the bloodshed," Holmes stated.

"Many of these internationalists established relationships with localites like the bankers and financiers," Watson added.

"So, after the Duke left, the Nazis were already plugged into the system," Hunter suggested.

"Exactly," Holmes said.

"I still don't see a problem," I said.

"Well, for years Nazis have been parlaying these relationships to fund Nazi businesses in Argentina. It has been assumed that the Crown approved this business, but truth is they didn't even know about it. That's according to insiders. And Mycroft would never deceive me."

"It's still a little vague to me too, sir," Hunter said. "What are we supposed to do now?" It can't be much of a situation all these years later."

"But it is, I'm afraid."

"The Bank of Europe-America (BEA) was taken over by a consortium of investors from Europe and the Bahamas," Holmes said "All of the investors on both sides of the ocean have Nazi ties."

"There are hundreds of banks in the Bahamas because the laws allow foreign companies a tax haven as an international business company (IBC). This bank (BEA) is just one of them. As long as they pay their licensing fees and government assessments they will stay in business. And they will continue to bail out and fund Nazi projects in South America. To date most of BEA money has gone to Argentina. But that is about to change. A major expansion is being planned to spread funds throughout South and Central America. The goal is to destabilize the regions and thereby create opportunity for a whole new fascist front."

"Hunter, you are right. This is just wild and hard to believe," I said.

"Well, I have a plan and Tom thinks it will work. We stay with our previous identities and approach BEA for loans to support and build German Culture Centers in several cities in Chile, Paraguay, Peru and Venezuela in South America. In Central America, we will set up in Costa Rica and British Honduras."

"This is starting to sound like California where the city park was a German cultural center but later became a meeting and training facility for young Nazis," Hunter said.

"That's the basic idea," Watson said. "Once these centers are located, they will declare their true loyalties and political preferences. All of these projects will market and advertise with large signs that they are being funded and sponsored by Bank of Europe-America (BEA) of Bahamas."

"That sounds like we will need a lot of manpower," I said.

"We will have all we need, Tom assures me," Holmes said.

"But we probably won't need it. We'll rent properties in various cities in all of the countries we have selected and put up signs for expected development and building plans with 'BEA Financing,'" Watson explained. "Anyway, our plan will expose BEA before there is any real construction or spending. We will post enough manifestos of fascist nonsense that even Hitler's generals would think they were too extreme for public consumption."

"Yes, that is wild, Watson," Hunter said. "But I like it."

"It gets better," Holmes said. "We will disclose the source of our creditworthiness to BEA as being derived from the art sales. If we need verification we will provide statements from the Boudreaux boys. And we can identify some of our upcoming black-market art sales recently discussed with Otto. Once they see what art work we are buying and selling they will know that we are involved in Nazi looted art. We will explain we don't really need their money but it looks good for our businesses to have development loans. Our reputation is important as we are working with new charter members of the Organization of American States (OAS), the leading regional organization for South and Central America. At the same time, we can offer to provide no interest loans of cash to BEA from our upcoming sales. We are expecting to have a problem with excessive cash very soon, and therefore we need to borrow funds to keep our businesses looking above board and beyond any suspicion," Holmes explained.

"Well, Count Felix Von Kramm, you and Tom have come up with a masterful plan," Hunter said.

"That's right," Watson said. "Chase Manhattan Bank of New York is working with MI5 and the Financial Crimes Unit (FCU), thereby getting us guarantees from Chase Manhattan Bank for any sums we want from BEA. We will be asking for ten million dollars for each project in ten different cities."

"And they will loan the money because of the Chase guarantee?" I asked. "That means Tom and David R. of the Bank are working behind the scenes."

"There are many actors working behind the scenes," Holmes said. "We will be centerstage, boys."

"Wow," Hunter said. "Thank God we have been learning the trade from the best Nazi hunters in the world. That includes both of you"

"Thank you," Holmes said.

"Yes, yes," Watson agreed.

All of the arrangements were made for our meetings in the Bahamas with the BEA. The advance work done by MI5 (*Regnum Defende*-Defend the Realm) and MI6 (*Semper Occultus*-Always Secret) was seamless and perfectly staged.

The four of us traveled to the Bahamas to put the deal together. Watson was identified as an associate of Count Felix and a *charge d'affaires* for an unidentified embassy mission. Watson was very excited to confront Nazis with a refusal to say what diplomatic minister or ambassador he was affiliated with.

"I will make it clear that my position is classified and secret and I will die before disclosing the nature of my work."

Bahamas banker Jerome Kleindeinst, President, BEA, told Mr. Audi Walkenhauser (Watson): "I respect your need for privacy, sir. This illustrates the problem today in banking and government disclosure. Our privacy is not respected. But here, sir, we admire your commitment to privacy and honor."

"I am glad because if there would be a problem, we would just go to one of the other twenty banks in the Bahamas recommended to us as being business friendly to international art business people."

"No need, sir. No need at all. This will be your bank. BEA wants your business and we will work to keep it. All of your plans are fully supported by BEA. Your Cultural Affair Institute is the type of business we wish to partner with throughout South and Central America."

"In the future we will expand to include cultural offices for Italy, Spain and England. The world needs to know about the failure of democratic governments everywhere they exist. We will always advocate for nationalism and freedom," Count Felix told the bank president and his assistants Hans Mueller and Wilson Ludendorff.

The bankers couldn't wait to issue funds to us. They knew these loans would provide them a source for endless amounts of cash at no cost from our profits derived from art sales. It was amazing how few questions were asked regarding our multi-city buildout. The biggest problem for us was getting the funds in the right type of accounts.

Eventually, we used ten separate development accounts. Funds were deposited into all accounts for the total loan value of ten million dollars each. Over the next two weeks arrangements were made with our "Swiss" bankers (MI5, FCU) for bank to bank transfers.

Just like that. Poof! The money from BEA was gone. And BEA officials were happy to make ten large loans that would never be repaid.

Our work was done. We did the set up. The FCU (Financial Crimes Unit) of MI5 would do the take down.

Holmes debriefed brother Mycroft when we returned to London. Although we were not involved in that session, Holmes and Watson did present us with medals of appreciation from the British Government.

The medals were similar to the ones we received from the Mossad agents we had worked with. Each medal was in a box fit for jewels and was the size of a silver dollar. There was an outline of Parliament on one side and the other side had the words "Strength and Honor" on the coin.

Just like before, we gave the medals to Tom. "Perhaps you could send on to David R. in New York," I said.

Tom advised that BEA had become a part of a huge banking scandal among the offshore banks outside of America.

"We got rid of the known Nazis, but of course there are other unscrupulous bankers who will fund Nazi inspired businesses in South America. They will now be on the radar screen. For the time being, BEA is dead and the British government is very thankful for your prompt success on this mission."

CHAPTER 4

MONUMENTS WOMEN

"**WE HAVE A NEW PROBLEM** with Nazis in Ireland," Tom said.

"That doesn't sound quite right," Hunter said.

"Mr. Holmes has been contacted by a leading archivist in London who worked in Europe after the war tracking down stolen art and returning works to owners or families of owners. She was part of the Monuments Men. She was the leading Monuments Woman. Although her Nazi tracking work has officially ended, she does maintain contact with sources in Europe she developed while working with the Monuments Men."

"Holmes will fill you in on details. Be safe. Ireland is a funny place."

After leaving Tom, Hunter wanted to know what I thought Tom meant in his comment about Ireland. I could only guess that he was referring to Ireland's neutrality during World War II. Also, there had been reports over the years after the war that Nazi military leaders found refuge in Ireland.

"That's crazy," Hunter said. "All my Irish friends hate Nazis like we do."

"Well, Hunter, some Irish believed the old adage that the enemy of my enemy is my friend. Since England was looked upon by some Irish as an enemy, well, you now the rest."

"Still, it makes no sense to give cover to Nazis in Ireland," Hunter repeated.

Tom was right. Holmes knew all the details. The whys and the wherefores.

"One of the great women of London is Anne Olivier Bell. She was one of very few women recruited for Monuments Men duties at the end of the war. She was well known in England as a member of the Bloomsbury group."

"They were like Hemingway's group in France, weren't they?" Hunter asked.

"Similar, similar," Watson said. "They were all a little rebellious in their thinking. Free thinkers."

"Well, Watson, to be fair, there were some brilliant minds too. John Maynard Keynes for one. Virginia Woolf another."

"Yes, of course, there were many brilliant English writers, philosophers and artists who gathered at the home of Clive and Vanessa Bell in the Bloomsbury district of London near the British Museum."

"And sometimes Bertrand Russell, Aldous Huxley and T.S. Elliot were associated with the Bloomsbury set," Holmes said.

"Well, I would say Hemingway would fit right in with that bunch," Hunter said. "He could hold his own with the big shot intellectuals."

"I never met the man, but I have read about his exploits around the world," Holmes said. "I believe you're right Hunter. He could hold his own with the Bloomsbury group. I'm sure he probably knew many of them."

"That's probably right about Hemingway," I said. "We have worked with him tracking Nazis in America and Cuba. He was part of the 'Lost Generation' in Paris in the 1920's. That was quite a bunch."

"And there were some of the Bloomsbury set in Hemingway's Lost Generation," Hunter said. "Virginia Woolf, TS Elliot, Huxley."

"According to Anne Bell, Nazis recently moved stolen works of art into some caves in County Tipperary, near Mitchelstown.

"This area of Ireland is known as the Ancient East," Watson said. "The Nazis believed the Vikings used the caves to hide loot while they carried out their rampaging and pillaging. No one knows if that's true, but when did Nazis ever worry about truth."

"Exactly, Watson. Exactly. Our job is to go to Cork and meet with our Irish contacts which include the Directorate of Military Intelligence and members of the Irish Army Ranger Wing (ARW)."

"Oh, those guys, yeah. *Remember the Name*," Hunter said. "I've heard of the A.R.W. They will become the special operations unit of the Irish Army someday. For now, they are considered an experimental military project."

"That's it precisely, Hunter," Holmes said. "They don't really exist, except for secret missions like this."

"The backstory has to do with Anne Bell still trying to find stolen art, although the war ended more than ten years ago. She just never gives up. Her method of pursuit is to contact art merchants throughout Europe offering to buy art for private collections. Her card reads:

Ann Bovard Nelson
Art Agent
Private Sales Only
London, Paris, Rome

"As a result, she gets calls several times a year. Most are small estate inquiries, but once in a while calls are about private collections. That is when Anne reaches out to Tom. That is the case here.

"I'm going to Ireland with you," Holmes said. "Watson will stay in London to finish some business with my brother's people.

"When we are ready to go meet the Nazis in Ireland, Anne will make contact to work out the details. I'm her liaison. I intend to be a businessman on this work. We will leave the Count here in England with Watson. I own gold mines in Africa and I am from South Africa and my name is Rudolf van der Kaap. Our family is known throughout the diamond world. Everyone knows there are accusations that our family traffics in blood diamonds which finance wars and warlords. Any Nazi would enjoy doing business with a predator like me."

"Mr. Holmes, we have never known you to be so nefarious, even odious," I said.

"Yeah, and so badass," Hunter added.

"Badass. I like that, Hunter."

"Holmes, you lecture me on decorum and here you are talking like a repeat customer down at the Old Bailey (Criminal Courts-London)," Watson said.

"Dear Watson, you are right, generally. But we are dealing with the lowest form of criminal. These people are amoral. I need to be the most badass I can be."

"I see."

"Boys, I always try to get into character. There are days I wish I would have dedicated myself to acting. I could play Shakespeare roles every day of my life. Hunter, you said you and your brother studied my disguises. The drunkard was one. And the man with the twisted lip. That required getting in character. I've been a priest, a nobleman, a masked burglar. I was even an Irish-American spy. The role required I learn a good deal of American slang. So, Watson, I will study the lingo of the South African diamond trade and that will support my disguise."

"Anne Bell (aka Ann Bovard Nelson-Private Art Sales) is going to take care of introductions for us. She will be assisted by Lady Lynn Nicholas who is a world-renowned expert on the subject of Nazi theft of art. They have both met me before when I was in disguise. This time will be no different. Of course, it helps me with my cover having a brother at a high level in the British Government. Mycroft dear Mycroft.

"Mycroft has arranged to have Rudolph van der Kaap (me) meet these lead players before we all go to Ireland.

"You should have seen the look on his face when I advised we should meet at the Diogenes Club in London. I told him it was necessary for security reasons. He has agreed and so maybe we can put an end to Diogenes being a gentlemen only club."

"Good job," Hunter said. "Some of these English customs are archaic and don't have much value in the twentieth century."

Hunter and I were anticipating a little flare up in the lobby of the Diogenes Club, but nothing happened.

"I thought the men-only rule would cause a problem, Mr. van der Kaap," I said.

"Social change is afoot, I'm sure. Even in old England."

"It's about time," Anne Bell said.

"I will second that," Lady Lynn agreed.

At that time Hunter pulled me aside and told me one of the rules of membership is that no club member is permitted to pay any notice to any other member and since we were taken to the club by Mycroft (Sir John Beasley), we were not even noticed.

"Thank you Mr. van der Kaap for helping us put these Nazis out of business," Anne Bell said. "Tom said you were the man for this job."

"Thank you. Tom and I have worked on several Nazi take-downs, huh?"

"Yes, we know, and we are so fortunate that you will join us," Lady Lynn Nicholas said.

"It will be my honor, yeah? To work with Monuments Women, yeah? Dem Nazis will be sorry they ever met the likes of you, ja, ja."

At that moment Hunter appeared to sneeze and his glass of water went flying. But he did not sneeze. I've seen this move before. It happens whenever Hunter gets flabbergasted. And after hearing Holmes as van der Kaap, Hunter cracked up, but gracefully covered his laughter with sneezing.

"My God Jordan, he had me convinced he is a South African diamond man," Hunter whispered.

"I'm sure these Nazis will eat out of your hand Rudolph," Lady Lynn said.

"And I got my boys with me, Hunter and Jordan. They're learning the trade, ja. I recruited them from America because they have experience hunting alligators, huh"

"I'm not sure that makes any sense, sir," Anne Bell said.

"That's what we both said," Hunter remarked. "But Tom and Rudolph said it made perfect sense."

"Okay, Okay. Let's put this plan together," Lady Lynn demanded. And then we did. It was an awesome plan.

Sir John Beasley (Mycroft) was able to arrange military transport (RAF) to Cork, Ireland the following Friday. We were scheduled to meet the gatekeepers for the Nazi gangsters near the Mitchelstown Caves.

The meeting was set for 3 pm at a farmhouse one mile from the cave entrance. Hans Bismarck was the contact man. He assured Art Agent Ann Bovard Nelson that they would be prepared to make deals at that time, so come prepared.

Sir John Beasley brought a small sack of lookalike diamonds that were used by gemologists for teaching. In particular, the stones were exact replicas of famous diamonds which are part of the Crown Jewel collection at the Tower of London.

"These are high quality replicas of the Cullinan white cut diamond from South Africa and the Koh-i-Nur diamond of India."

"That is excellent," Anne Bell said. "The Koh-i-Nur is good luck to women and bad luck to men."

"Of course, friends, the Cullinan diamond is the largest uncut diamond ever, and I will be glad to tell the Nazis all about it," van der Kaap (S. Holmes) said.

"You will have your day, you will," Hunter said. "Yeah?"

"I believe he is right, bru," I said.

"My, my," Anne Bell said. "They are all getting on the South African lingo train."

When we arrived at the designated farmhouse, we were greeted by a local farmer who seemed to have no knowledge about Nazis or art.

"If you're the folks wishin' to meet the German man, he is up the road at the Thomastown Castle. You know, the castle was in bad shape before, but your man has done a fine job bringing the old place back," Mr. Matt Fogarty explained. "He's not a horseman, so none of us know what he is doing in Tipperary country. We are just glad he fixed up the place.

"And he's a private man. Not one Irish person is employed on the estate. That is a little bit of a problem because some folks, including me, think there might be some shenanigans going on and possibly something worse."

"Sir, Mr. Fogarty, you might as well know that Bismarck is a strange man," Anne Bell said. "We believe he is a Nazi and a thief on a grand scale. He is also probably dangerous. Please keep this information to yourself until we can apprehend him on criminal charges."

"Yes, Miss Anne, good to know. Bless you for what you're doing. We have no need for Nazis or thieves in Ireland."

"What about the caves?" I asked. "What is he doing there, bru?"

"Nothing yet. He wants to store some old family furniture received from his recently deceased mother in Germany. He said his mother was Irish who married a German man. So the story went. The furniture has been arriving for weeks and it will soon go to the caves for storage. I'm not sure if the widow Mulcahy would really rent cave space for storage. If she does it's probably only in the Old Desmond cave which is closed to the public anyway."

"Why is that, huh?"

"It's dangerous as there's a one hundred foot drop off by the entrance."

"Where do we go to first, Mr. Fogarty?" Anne Bell asked.

"I'm supposed to take you to the Thomastown Castle first, but I can show you the caves if you wish."

"Great idea. We'll do that."

The purpose in going to see the caves was to confirm the presence of Irish Army Ranger Wing. We saw no sign of the ARW but Anne recognized civilians on the property as being Irish Military Intelligence. We merely waved at them and gave a tip of the hat. Anne said everyone was in place and ready, so then we went to the castle.

Anne rode with Mr. Fogarty and we followed behind them.

Upon arriving at the Thomastown Castle, we spotted Bismarck immediately. We were all stunned seeing this middle-aged man on the front steps of the castle tower wearing what looked like a World War I Prussian Cavalry tunic uniform.

Bismarck approached our vehicles and welcomed the entourage. Anne Bell did the "alias" introductions for our bunch.

"The Boudreaux boys from Louisiana working with the famous diamond family of South Africa. Now I've heard everything," Hans Bismarck said.

"I hope we're not late for the battle, bru," Hunter said. Everyone froze for a few seconds then Bismarck started laughing hysterically. All I could think was this was classic Hunter. We all laughed.

"I wear this uniform to honor my namesake and distant relative, Otto von Bismarck. He was the first Chancellor of Germany and a real statesman."

"I know he was a prince and even a duke, but I don't remember him being a soldier," Hunter responded.

"I will check on that Mr. Boudreaux. I know he was in the army for a while."

"He certainly led the military in several moves to unify Germany. He said forget the speeches we need iron and blood. The Iron Chancellor, yeah?"

"Very good, Fabian Boudreaux. It sounds like you're a student of the unification of Germany and history of 19th Century Europe."

"Well, ja, I studied the formation of the German state and how it led to World War I and then how that led to World War II."

"We could talk this history for hours but I think our friends want to discuss art, not world diplomacy."

"Of course, bru," Hunter agreed.

"Well, proceed sir," Ann Bovard Nelson said. "We are here to buy. My client, Mr. van der Kaap of South Africa has brought some valuable stones to establish his good faith."

"Thank you, Rudolph, sir. I would love to see your South African treasures."

"This is one of the nine Cullinan Diamonds, yeah?" van der Kaap said. "We got to keep one after it was cut. Cullinan is the largest diamond ever found and is now part of the Crown Jewels, except this one. It was found on our property in South Africa, yeah? I also brought a Koh-i-Nur diamond which comes from Persia, huh? Likewise, this diamond was with the Crown Jewels of England, bru. But it has gone missing and here it is!

"What I'm saying, bru, is we're worth dealing with. Dem diamonds are kief," van der Kaap said.

"That means awesome," Hunter said.

"Yes, they are," Bismarck said.

"Your call, Hans. Do we stay here or go to the caves to see what you want to sell?" Ann asked.

"We haven't moved the art to the caves yet. We have been setting up in this old mansion. We have divided the artists by nationality to simplify things. Most everything I have is modern. We have a few famous masters.

"These are mainly artists known by collectors and those who have special interests.

"In the Library are the French painters:

Franz Marc	Henri Monnier
Henri Matisse	Constantin Guys
Camille Roqueplan	Pierre Auguste Renoir
Pierre Bonnard	Pierre-Jules Méne
Edouard Manet	Jean-Louis Forain
Camille Pissaro	Picasso
Paul Signac	Claude Monet
Edouard Manet	

"In the Drawing Room are the Polish artists:

Josef Simmler	Veit Stoss
Ludwig Buchhorn	Henri Gervex
Henryk Siemiradzki	Jan Matejko

"The Dutch are in the Dining Hall:

Joris van der Haagen

Haagse Bos

Hans Memling

Wassily Kandinsky

Jan Adam Kruseman

The Dining Hall is the largest room in the house. That room has one classic old-world painting which is of the lord of this manor. I am told it is a portrait of the lawyer for Henry VIII. Besides being busy with all the domestic disputes, he apparently was a very successful lawyer. This is a stately home, and it is perfect for showing art. Whatever doesn't sell here will go to the Mitchelstown Caves for safe storage with around the clock guards just like a museum, except it will be even more secure."

"I know we are your first client visitors, which I appreciate," Ann Bovard Nelson said.

"You have been a good customer with us for several years now. We believe you deserved to be first to see this magnificent collection we have been privileged to show and sell. No one has seen these works since the war."

"You mean since they disappeared?" Hunter said with some attitude.

"My son," van der Kaap said, "that is the nature of war. Things go missing, you know, the spoils of war. Since time immemorial, huh?"

"Maybe he's right cousin, ja," I said. "Wars cause people to take things from the enemy."

"Ok," Hunter said. "But who was the enemy? The artists? "I don't know. I guess I don't get it."

A knock on the door broke up the awkward moment.

"I'm Colonel Michael Hourigan, Director of Military Intelligence in Ireland. The men behind me are all with the Army Ranger Wing. Although these members of ARW have their weapons drawn, they have been instructed not to engage unless a threat is realized. Anyone here with a weapon, please put it on the floor in front of you."

"What is this home invasion about? Are you some sort of Irish Nazi sir?"

"Mr. Bismarck, we have been watching your shipments coming into Cork Harbor for the last several months and we think you are stockpiling some type of contraband."

"I assure you, Colonel, we have no contraband. Look around."

"Men, take Mr. Bismarck into custody. Take the rest of them into that large room and get identification from all of them. What are they doing here? Find out."

"They are here to buy art. That is not a crime, Colonel."

"True, as long as everything is legit, sir. But I'm inclined to think this art is stolen. That will be confirmed as we will soon be joined by my colleague from the Secret Intelligence Service (MI6) in England, Francis Ponsonby."

"We can take the smuggler in chief to Cork where we have secure facilities that can handle international criminal and syndicate members," Hourigan said.

"I hope the facility can handle Nazis because I think that's what we're dealing with," Ponsonby said. "All this art must be stolen and it could only come from one source, Nazis."

"We have with us members of the Monuments Men team from England who will check out all of the paintings which seem to be on display in every room of this mansion. There must be hundreds—all of them by famous artists, most of whom were banished or worse by the Nazis. (Bell and Nicholas were not identified as the experts as there was no reason to disclose their true identities, just in case something would go wrong with the arrest. They would remain suspects along with the rest of the bunch).

"Well, Mr. Fogarty, you can let any future visitors here at Thomastown Castle know that Hans Bismarck will be in the sneezer down in Cork. He'll have his own room at the greybar hotel," Hourigan said.

"Keeping him at the Calaboose hoosegow?" Fogarty asked.

"We will for a while," MI6 Ponsonby added. "Once the Irish Military Intelligence has processed Bismarck, the boys with the Ranger Wing will escort Bismarck to England where a system is in place to prosecute Nazis who are selling stolen art and such."

Hunter, Holmes and I walked away from the castle down through a thick boreen (path) that hadn't been traveled in years. As we looked back at the castle, we admired the architectural beauty of the place.

"Yes, it is a magnificent work of architecture," Holmes said. "The shame, indeed the crime, is the desecration in so many respects by this Nazi syndicate. Our humanity is on the line. This war with Nazis is not over. It may never end. The Holocaust has ended for now. But we cannot assume it is over for all time. No, vigilance is our duty now and forever."

"Amen." Hunter lifted his clasped hands to the sky.

And then the Nazi Bismarck was gone. The art works would be secured by a professional team from the continent and placed in official repositories in their home countries.

We returned to England with Holmes and brother Mycroft (Sir John Beasley). The Monuments Women remained behind to work with the art specialists and all others. Basically, Anne Bell and Lady Lynn Nicholas were in charge of the art at a major crime scene.

Hourigan told us they had names of other Nazis involved with Bismarck. He said they would attempt to work with Bismarck to get him to give up his partners in crime. Giving good information would be helpful for Bismarck at his sentencing at the Old Bailey in London, he was told. If direct evidence of genocide was related to these thefts then the whole matter could be transferred to the International Criminal Court in the Hague, Netherlands. To be determined.

As usual, at the end of our hunt for the particular Nazi(s), we left the scene of the crime with no prisoners in tow. But we weren't policeman, Holmes reminded us. "That's the job of the police and the legal system," he said. "That's the way it has to be. They have their job to do when we complete our work. You'll get used to it. Most of the time the system works."

"Guess you're right," Hunter said. "I'm not going to be a cop or FBI Agent. I'm doing what we said we would do. We told sister we would track down Nazis, and that is what we are doing. We are seeking justice for her and all the people who lost their family members and their worldly possessions."

"That's right. It is how it must be, men. We have to do our work so that the police and various authorities can lock up these war criminals and Nazis."

"I agree, Mr. Holmes," I said.

"I must say, brother, that was said eloquently and to the point," Mycroft said.

"Well, we will be in England again soon. I am always thankful to make it back home. I will immediately brief Watson on our success. And, I assume you will see Tom as soon as you can."

"Thank you, sir, for the help in preparing us for being from South Africa. We look forward to more such work, huh?" Hunter said.

"And thanks for helping me be a badass. I needed that coaching."

"You're alright, bru."

The discussion on the way home was focused on the desire of all of us for some rest and peace and quiet. But it was just talk. We were too amped up to rest. This effort with Mr. Holmes was a major accomplishment for us. Anyway you look at it. We got better because of the assistance of the master sleuth and we got first class training in acting and performance. Holmes was good, but he cautioned us to be humble when going undercover, whether in disguise or not.

"Just remember, Hunter and Jordan, I wasn't such a badass when I tried to outsmart Irene Adler. She got the best of me and I will never forget the schooling I got from that young lady. Even dear Watson said I was defeated by a woman's wit and it's true. I was. So, just remember, always be respectful of the mind of women. It is a lesson I learned the hard way in *Scandal in Bohemia*. Irene Adler established that men have no lock on logic and reason in the execution of an undercover plan."

"We are warned," I said.

"I agree Mr. Holmes," Hunter said. "My mother convinced me about the power of the brain of women. I am still learning from her every day. As I look back on my youth, I realize she was always right and I was generally on the other side of the equation. My salvation is that I realize the errors of my ways. Sir, you are so right."

We would soon say our goodbyes and go to meet with Tom for a debriefing and find out what mission was next.

CHAPTER 5

THE VICHY SQUAD

"Tom, we had great success in Ireland and can give you a quick or detailed report," I said.

"Not now, Jordan. We have a problem on the continent. Worse yet, it is back home in France. I am ashamed to admit that Nazis have been transacting their business and activities in all the major cities of France."

"Tom, you have taught us to believe Nazis can be anywhere in this big world," Hunter said. "That's why you are here and why we are here. We will go wherever we need to go. That includes France."

"Yes, yes, you're right, but it hurts to think they are still in my homeland. We did so much work with the Resistance and the Allied troops to get rid of the Nazis in France."

"What is the problem?" I asked. "Who and where? What do you want us to do?"

"Back in 1944, after D-Day, we pushed the Vichy squads out of France and into Sigmaringen, Germany. Of course, we supported Free France with General de Gaulle. Other Vichy French left France to avoid being prosecuted for treason and war crimes, since they sent many French Jews to the concentration camps."

"I know the story only too well, Tom. My parents had friends in France who didn't make it," I said.

"Tom, I knew that Marshal Philippe Petain was the head of Vichy France," Hunter said. "And he colluded with the German Nazis."

"That's exactly, right, Hunter. But we have underestimated the amount of corruption that continues to this day."

"Tom, I firmly believe that fifty years from now we will still be hunting down Nazis who stole art from Jewish families or acquired paintings through forced sales," Hunter said.

"I find that hard to accept, but I'm afraid you may be right."

"That's the problem here. Black-market sales of Nazi looted art. All of this is done through a group of high-end hotels in all of the major French cities:

Nice

Lyon

Paris

Bordeaux

Marseille

Avignon

Dijon

Aix-en-Provence

Caen

Toulouse

These ex-Vichy collaborators have been acquiring a lot of stolen art since the end of the war. Their plan has been to present evidence of ownership to museums and government art repositories. They have acquired a vast collection worth a fortune.

"How could they fake ownership?" I asked.

"Let me put it this way. They knew the owners because they stole it during the war. Then when this art was retrieved after the war, it was sent to safe places or placed under government supervision. These French Nazis knew what evidence of ownership was needed for thousands of works of art."

"So, they stole the art a second time," I said.

"Exactly."

"This is really bad, Tom," Hunter said.

"It sounds like a floating crap game," I said. "They just keep moving the black-market sales game to the next town. All in France and all by Frenchmen."

"That is why I am having a difficult time coming to terms with the whole ordeal."

"My presence would cause them to shut down, so I need to stay clear of France for now."

"I guess the Boudreaux boys will be called back into action again," Hunter said.

"It is becoming a comfortable alias identity," I admitted.

Aix en Provence

Tom gave us the full brief on the French Nazis. We didn't know what to call them as a group so we decided to call them the Vichy Squad. And they became the target.

Holmes would not be part of this take-down unless he was needed in an emergency. Tom said Holmes was working with brother Mycroft for a few weeks on some urgent matters of state.

We were told what upcoming black-market sales were coming soon and we were told to pick the city to start our mission.

"That's easy, Tom," Hunter said. "It has to be Aix en Provence, the home of Paul Cézanne."

"What's with Aix en Provence?" I asked.

"Just some place I have always wanted to go to. I read about it and wanted to go to university there. But it was just a pipedream. I didn't have the money. It was an illusion. Or maybe it wasn't. I can finally go there. We have to have our dreams."

"I get it, Hunter," Tom said. "Those thoughts still haunt me. My dreams."

"I am not haunted by the past. I just want to help make things better today. Aix en Provence was always a positive dream. I now get to go there and make the world a better place. That's awesome, Tom."

"You're right, Hunter. I'm just being sad for no good reason."

"It's okay Tom," I said. "We all have our sad memories, but we will triumph. Hunter and I will take justice to the Vichy Squad. It will be an honor to carry out this mission. We do this for you and for France."

"I will reach out to some of my former Resistance brothers and sisters to let them know we may need their help."

"Excellent. We will start to prepare. Let us know when we need to be in France."

"Details to follow soon, boys. Now that we have selected a location, the plan will come together soon."

"We will let Mr. Holmes know what and where, just in case we need his help," Hunter said.

"Agree."

We were scheduled to meet our contact near Gare d'Aix en Provence—the rail station. Our hotel was small and uncomfortable, but close to where the action would be.

For the meeting with our local Resistance contact "Nichelieu" we would meet in a local cafe. She basically only used her last name, Tom told us. Her first name was Gabrielle, but in the Resistance she was known as Angel. Her namesake was the famous archangel.

The cafe was very small and had no name, which is how we found it. It was located in the center of town on the *Place de la Rotonde*.

"I'm Nichelieu, gentlemen. Tom probably said I had no first name. That was true in the past but I am happy to be called Angel. No Nazis are chasing me now, although possibly that might be changing I've been told."

"It is an honor to meet you," Hunter said.

"Yes, a real honor Miss Angel," I said.

"And I feel the same," she said. "You boys remind me of my comrades in the Resistance during the war. There were many young men and women like me fighting the Nazis who stole our country back then. Today, that spirit is gone, and I'm afraid we French have let our guard down."

"Well, we are here to reestablish that *esprit de corps*," Hunter said.

"*Merci, merci.*"

"Hunter is right. We need to bring back that feeling of fighting together for right. For morality," I said.

"We need some privacy to meet and discuss things. Before leaving the *Fontaine de la Rotonde*, I need to show you the sculpture that surrounds the fountain. Besides the lions and swans, you can see the angels on the backs of the dolphins. And above the angels are the Women of Justice and Art. The symbolism is not just a coincidence. We are here for a purpose that is bigger than any one person or thing. Look at her. Madame Justice."

"Enough said," Hunter said. "Your place or ours?"

"Our hotel room is pretty small," I said.

"We can go to my hotel. I have plenty of room with extra space for you to stay also. Tom has worked his usual hotel magic. I have a top floor suite with balcony overlooking the *Cours Mirabeau*. The ceilings are plasterwork showing angels. It is all meant to be."

"You're right. Tom has the hotel magic hand," Hunter said.

"My hotel has a long French name, but most people just call it Hotel de Villars."

An Edith Piaf classic was being performed by a young singer in the lobby of the hotel. She was accompanied by a piano man old enough to be her grandfather. Maybe he was. She beautifully sang the song "*Je Ne Regrette Rien.*"

"That's how we feel, Angel," Hunter said. "We have no regrets. Right Jordan?"

"Just like Edith said. No regrets."

"Well, you should have no regrets. It sounds like the operation at the Irish caves went well. Anne Bell and Lady Lynn Nicholas have been true pioneers in the battle to recover art and treasure stolen by the Nazis. And Rudolph van der Kaap has quite the reputation for taking chaos to the Nazis."

"Do you know him?" I asked.

"I'm not sure anyone really knows him. I think he is in disguise most of the time. In recent times we worked together once in South Africa. Of course, we had help from him during the war. He looked different every time I saw him. He is obsessed with and destined to be a master of disguise."

"It seems to work for him," Hunter said.

"Indeed," I said.

"I know he was a close friend of Tom's. We were told if we ever had serious problems with our missions that we could call Tom for the help of his friend, Mr. H. That's it. That's all we knew.

"A lot of us had secret identities and false identification in case we were caught and tortured. If I didn't know my fellow saboteur, it would be impossible to give him or her up to the Nazis.

"No one knew my last name, but somehow the Vichy French found out I was Nichelieu and they had me targeted. It was really bad because I was a woman. The Nazis were infuriated by that fact alone. How could a woman overpower a strong Aryan man? Easy, I outsmarted them. But enough about me. I am what I am. Somewhat damaged goods. I'm okay now but I was a heroin addict for a few years after the war. I lost my identity after the war. Once it ended, I ended."

"Well, Angel, we are living proof the war is not over," Hunter said. "Really, it will never end. There will always be a battle between good and evil. Here we are."

"I'm glad you put your life back together," I said.

"Mr. H. helped me tremendously. Tom sent him to help me when I hit bottom. He said he had experience with the same thing, addiction. That was all I needed. I've been back to the world since then.

I work all of Europe, the Middle East and Africa for Tom. The battle goes on even after the war ended. Just like you're saying."

"What about Mr. H?" Hunter asked.

"I don't know. He was like a father I never had and yet he was like a friend. He did everything to help me come back and get away from the habit that would have killed me. So, you see, I owe Tom my life. And Mr. H. Since he has no name, I always thought he was a British spy. That's okay. He was there for me. That's all that matters."

"Wow, that's quite a story, Angel," I said.

"We all owe thanks to Tom and Mr. H.," Hunter said. "We think of him as our Sherlock Holmes. He's always there to save the day. Just like Holmes."

"That's funny. That's how I always think of him. He's like a modern-day Sherlock Holmes. No doubt inspired by the great detective and just as secretive."

"Sounds like we all agree that Mr. H. is our version of Holmes," I said.

"When we had a bad day he used to say: 'Well, Watson, we seem to have fallen upon evil days.'"

"Same here," I said.

"That's right," Hunter said. "Watson was always there. Never forgotten."

"Well, back to the drawing table, Angel. What we have with this Vichy Squad is their stolen art version of a floating crap game. And the art is the float. They move from city to city. Always in first class hotels and always private sales. Very stealthlike. All hotel staff are paid off to keep the business quiet. It is a super silent black-market. They have been operating full time for a year now. Tom has done the provenance research and investigation so we know the where and the when. We know some of the who's. More importantly, they know us from the art world black-market. We are becoming known. We are the Boudreaux boys of Switzerland (by way of Louisiana). We have been dealing with a character who goes by the business names of Otto Muehlebach or Otto Brown. After the war he went to America with his brother Hans Von Krupp, a German rocket scientist who works for the Defense Department back home in the U.S.

"We are scheduled to meet with Mr. Wilson Klug at 2:00 pm at the Hotel Olivier," I said. "Clearly that is not his real name. It doesn't matter. We are in and you will be with us as our assistant and art advisor. This works good with your expertise in modern art. Like Nazis around the world, these Vichy Nazis are also unloading modern art. They are only buying masters or classic paintings."

"Why don't we work a trade?" Angel asked.

"What do you propose?" we asked.

"I'm sure you know the ploy. Our classics for your moderns. Let's make a deal."

"You're right, Angel. We have played this game before."

"Boys, we know what they want. The highest value masterworks in the world. The older the better. They'll lose money if they can get their inventory washed. Just like laundering money, except they're willing to wash the blood from their hands by selling the art stolen from people who died."

"So, Angel, we should put a list together of possible masterworks which are missing. We can use those for our trade talks. We've done this before but we weren't fully prepared. We need to do some research, Angel," I said.

"Well, boys, I'm up to speed. I even have a list of all valuable masterworks in the world that are missing due to theft or other nefarious reasons."

"That gives us two days to see the city I could not afford to visit in my youth," Hunter said. "Can we go see the art work of Paul Cezanne at one of the museums?"

"We can go see his studio. A friend of mine works there. It is now a museum. You will love it. Then we'll go to the Musée Granet where you can see even more of Mr. Cezanne. We can also see the permanent collection which features many works from antiquity and the Romans. Of course, Mr. Rembrandt is well represented there, as are many of the modern contemporaries: Picasso, Gauguin, Van Gogh, Matisse."

"I always remember that Hemingway said he learned about writing by studying the paintings of Cezanne."

"To change the subject a bit, if we go back to what we were talking about as far as the missing treasures, it is well known that when Berlin fell in Spring 1945 looters raided the Nazi Party Führerbau and stole all valuables, including nearly 1,000 paintings that were planned to go to the Führer museum in Linz, Austria. Some were recovered. Most weren't. Those are the treasures all Nazi thieves want. And I have lists of these works. We have collected all the information of original ownership, provenance, whether collector-owned or from private collections.

In an effort to maintain our credibility with this bunch I think we should focus on the art that belongs to Adolphe Schloss who had a huge private collection of Dutch and Flemish old masters. Nobody in the world knows the whereabouts of these paintings."

Saturday came very quickly, but we were ready. We reviewed endless lists of Nazi stolen art from all over Europe.

"They will press you on your knowledge and any information you boys have on the major works that are still missing."

"Like Raphael's Portrait of a Young Man," I said. "We faced those questions from Otto in Kansas City and Key West.

"We taunted him by saying we couldn't disclose names but we have viewed Raphael's masterpiece.

"I don't know what I was thinking. They could have kidnapped and tortured us for that information alone.

We know the major pieces still missing by artists Van Gogh, Klimt, Courbet, Schlüter, Bellini, Rembrandt."

"Don't forget Degas and the Five Dancing Women." Hunter said. "If we make any stupid mistakes, we'll be two dancing men, dancing to bullets being shot at our feet."

"No problem, boys. You're ready to tango with the Vichy Squad."

The Hotel Olivier

"Good afternoon," the hotel manager said. "How may we serve you today? *Puis-je vous aider?*"

"Your hotel badge says Wilson Klug. That is who we are here to meet," I said.

"You must be the Boudreaux boys of Louisiana and Switzerland."

"We are. I'm Fabian and this is Philly. Our assistant is Helene Hunziker of Switzerland."

"The hotel badge is just a prop. I like to know who is in the hotel during my business hours," Klug said.

"Klug sounds German, but your French is convincing," Fabian (Hunter) said.

"Well, good question. I'm like Kramer and Remarque from *All Quiet on the Western Front*."

"I'm Pierre Guillaume really. But Wilson is a good archetype German first name."

"Well, Pierre or Wilson, or whoever the hell you really are, that is the wackiest sidetrack explanation of an alias or aliases I have ever heard except for our buddy in high school, Jonny Conlee. He was always pretending to be a doctor or homicide detective. Never a hotel manager. We used to take our dates to a big fancy house to switch cars. It was actually the Archbishop's house and Jonny would prearrange to clean and wax the fancy church limo. Of course, he told our dates it was his mansion and his car."

"Fabian, this is a great story. Better than mine for sure."

"Were you part of this scheme Philly?"

"No sir. I never took dates home. Fabian had some weird friends in high school back in Louisiana."

"That's true, cuz," Fabian said.

"Excuse me gentlemen, but I was wondering if we are going to discuss art sales," Miss Hunziker queried.

"Yes, by all means we should discuss the topic of the day," Pierre said.

"But first I must ask you Fabian, if the girls believed Jonny lived in the mansion?"

"Every single time."

"That is amazing."

"When he told them his dumb white cat 'Cajun' was on the roof they would look up and see the cat. And the deal was sealed. That ceramic cat is still on the bishop's roof."

"Why did he want to be a detective if he was so successful with the mansion and limo?"

"Well, tell you the truth, he was pretty full of himself and thought he could pull off any ruse. You've got to understand Jonny was nearly seven feet tall and his ego was ten feet tall."

"How did he play homicide detective?"

"Well, he had me drive up to the movie theater in another church car, an all-black sedan. He would jump out and proclaim he was with homicide police and was investigating a murder. People cleared the way and he went in and sat in the mezzanine. Then shortly after the grand entrance I would call and tell the theater people I was the police station calling for homicide detective Conlee. And I ordered them to go get him at his mezzanine seat. I think you get the picture. He loved the attention. He loved himself. He should have run for Congress where he could have ended up with his own kind. Instead, he went to medical school, not to be a doctor but because he loved every nurse he ever met and he thought as a doctor he could meet and date more nurses. Well, it worked. He met a lot of nurses. He became a medical student. Then he died at age 25. Oversized body and undersized heart, they said."

"Wow, Fabian, that is a sad story," Pierre said.

"Not really. Jonny always said he'd be dead by age 30. He said the doctors called him a freak as a baby and child. His mother said he might die any day. So he said he was going to have serious fun every day. And he did. I wasn't sad when Jonny bit the dust. As they say back home in Louisiana, he probably died with a smile on his face. You know, he did it his way."

"I'm sorry Miss Helene Hunziker," Pierre said. "I'm exhausted emotionally just thinking about Fabian's friend Jonny. I say we get some drinks and then have dinner. We can do business tomorrow. I'm afraid I would not be very good at my job today. I just feel so bad for Jonny. He reminds me of my brother who died young. I try to forget, but this story brings back my own family tragedy."

"A couple drinks and a few bottles of wine will straighten you out, Pierre."

"You're right, Fabian."

Next day was down to business. We met at 9:00 am and everything went as planned. We offered to trade the famous missing collection of Dutch and Flemish masterworks. That was our offer and Pierre and associates were ecstatic. This would be the biggest deal of the year for the Vichy Squad.

We ironed out terms and conditions. Not much due diligence in this line of work. Crooks buying and selling to crooks.

The exchange of our classic masterworks for their famous modern paintings would take place in two days. The deal was our stash for theirs. They were told it would take us that long to get the paintings out of storage and packed and delivered to wherever they wanted them. They would inspect our trucks at the hotel loading dock and then advise for a warehouse drop-off point.

They agreed to do the same with their collection. We would meet at the hotel dock for a mutual inspection.

Pierre advised the next "meeting" place was the following week in Nice. We requested an introduction and appointment to see the inventory of Nice. Things were all lined up. We would meet Larrimore Montrose at the St. Patrice Hotel in Nice in one week.

Plenty of work to do before then.

The day before the meeting with Pierre we met for coffee and some French breakfast (Le Petit-dejeuner) in our hotel.

"Having coffee and p'tit dej, bra?"

"Good morning sir," Hunter said.

"Mr. Rudolph van der Kaap of South Africa this is Helene Hunziker of Switzerland."

"Oh my God. I barely recognize you," Angel said.

"I keep updating my South African vintage clothing. And, of course, when you deal with Nazis you have to take the personal stories over the top. They love the drama of personal grandiosity even if it makes no sense."

"It is good to see you H," Angel said as she reached across both of us to embrace the great detective. "I've missed you so much."

"We must get caught up after this work is done," Mr. H. said.

"I've decided to wear this Royal Military uniform because of my hereditary peerage as a Duke and Chief of Clan van der Kaap. I have the only legal private army in Europe, the Atholl Highlanders. Our clan was given this privilege by Queen Victoria in 1844, ja. So, that's what is going on in my life, yeah, how are you doing Miss Angel?"

"You are never simple, sir. I can only marvel at the lengths you go to in perpetuating a disguise."

"Thank you, dear. That is indeed a compliment coming from a master phantom, yeah."

"Sounds like a lot of history between you two," Hunter said.

"But we should probably put the plan together," I said.

"Yes, yes, of course you are right Jordan, bra."

"Tom sent me to help execute the plan. He has had some time to think about what to do. As for my uniform, it does have some relevance to this mission. We will need a small army to carry out this plan.

The small army is with me. It is an elite regiment of thirty members made up of soldiers from several European countries. They all trained in England with MI5 and MI6. This is very much like the new Army Ranger Wing (ARW) in Ireland we worked with recently. It is called Interpol Recovery Unit (IRU). All recoveries focus on stolen art and valuables. Most of the IRU work deals with family disputes at auctions and sales. But the joint command has been trained to activate and merge forces when called upon. Well, that call was made and the joint command operation is here in Aix en Provence at a nearby military storage annex. The colonel in charge is Fritz Papa of Berlin. That is the location where the crimes in this case took place."

"So, when do we meet these troops?" I asked.

"The plan is simple," Mr. H said. "We have two large lories which are made up to look like they contain and store paintings and valuable art.

"The goal is to get Pierre and his people inside the trailers to inspect the Adolphe Schloss collection. We expect to have the entire Vichy Squad at the hotel inside the units for inspection."

"At that point load and go?" Hunter asked.

"And the special forces will secure the Vichy inventory. The French Sûreté Nationale has been alerted to the operation which is expected to be a bloodless takedown," Mr. H. said.

"It sounds very clinical," Angel said. "Almost too clean."

"You may be right, Angel, but this is the plan and we will execute it in the morning."

Pierre will want to inspect the Adolphe Schloss Collection with his two expert art appraisers and he will assign lower-level assistants to show us the trade inventory to evaluate.

"Instead of inspecting art in the sound-proof cargo containers, they will be meeting the armed resistance of our soldier friends from the IRU. Armed troops will be inside the carrier containers.

"Basically, the plan covers all the contingencies we expect from the Vichy Squad," Mr. H. said.

Next day

"Good morning sir. You must be the Pierre I have heard so much about, and I am Rudolph van der Kaap of South Africa, ja. My clan is from the Atholl Highlands in Scotland originally. If you are curious about my outfit, Queen Victoria gave our clan the honor of this uniform I am wearing, bra."

"I don't follow exactly, sir."

"Well, our clan is in the diamond trade in South Africa, ja. We are dem boys what found the Great Cullinan, huh. The largest…"

"I know about that, sir. The largest ancient white diamond ever found. My God, Mr. van der Kaap, it is a wonderful honor," Pierre said.

"It is all starting to make sense. I didn't know how the Boudreaux boys would be able to generate the funds to put together this historic trade. But now I know. They represent the Lion of South Africa. Should I call you Duke Rudolph?" Pierre asked.

"I don't use that title unless I'm in Scotland. It is more like a hereditary quirk. Queen Victoria gave us a title and the right to raise an army, bra. It wasn't really an honor like people think. It was more like a concession to avoid war in 1844, yeah. Who cares, bru? She's dead and I got an army out of the deal. The only legal private army in Europe, huh. But, of course, I have the Atholl Highlanders in South Africa where I need them, bru."

"Amazing, sir. I look forward to visiting you in South Africa. Maybe more art deals in the future," Pierre said.

"Excellent, ja"

"Shall we look at inventory?" Helene suggested.

As we walked through the hotel kitchen area, we followed Pierre and assistants to the dock area behind the hotel where the trucks and trailers were located.

"Helene and I will go with Pierre. Boys you can go look at Pierre's art for trade and select what we want," Duke Rudolph said.

All of the trade art from Pierre was in a single trailer, also at the dock.

We said we would not enter Pierre's trailer until both of his groups were securely inside our cargo vessels at the dock. For security, they were told the doors needed to be securely closed. Then the clock began to run on finishing off the Vichy Squad. More agents of Interpol Recovery began arriving in military trucks. The men were in civilian dress but all displayed automatic weapons. The variety of weapons for this bunch was unmatched in modern non-combat military actions. The Pan-European force weapons included:

-FM 24/29 (French) light machine gun

- MG 24 (German) machine gun

-Bren gun (British) light machine gun

-ZB vz.26 (Czech) light machine gun

-M1924 (French) sub machine gun (killed Mussolini)

-MG 42 (German) the buzzsaw

-SE MAS (French) sub machine gun

Within minutes the trucks were commandeered by the Interpol force and taken directly to the military annex. Interpol took control of our vehicles and theirs. Theirs had the art. Ours had the criminals.

The next move would be to make contact with Nice. In an effort to get leniency Pierre agreed to notify his Nice associates that all went well and he would be out of communication for several days while taking inventory of the Adolphe Schloss Collection and verifying they got the entire collection. Pierre's note to Mr. Montrose in Nice read:

> Visitors will come to Nice soon. Hope you have as much success with your trades.

> Pierre

We met with Interpol commander Colonel Fritz Papa to review all details for the next black-market deal in one week in Nice. The set up in Nice was in place but we were not going to be needed. Essentially our takedown in Aix en Provence would make Nice an easy target. The rest of the Vichy Squad might get away and go underground. They would be back, of course. And so would we.

The Nazis would always want to trade or sell their stolen art. Time was on our side.

We said our goodbyes to friends and soldiers. Angel had been great to work with. We felt confident we would see her again.

"See you boys soon, I'm sure. Give my best to Tom. Mr. H, good to work with you as always."

Then Holmes and Angel stepped aside and had a parting embrace and that was it. Goodbye to Aix en Provence.

CHAPTER 6

TRACKING EICHMAN

ON OUR RETURN TO LONDON with Holmes we asked about his infamous adversary, the Professor. Was he real or just symbolic?

"People don't realize that I only met the man twice. He sure has gained a lot of notoriety for these brief encounters?"

"Let's see, sir, you met him at Baker Street once and the other meeting was at a location that presents one of the greatest dramatic scenes in all literature at Reichenbach Falls."

"Some day we can talk about that evil genius, but for now we have our work to do with the other evil degenerates that Hitler has spun off."

Holmes told us our next Nazi venue was going to be Argentina. Tom was gathering information and research from friends in Cuba who have pursued Nazis hiding in Argentina.

"You know Tom's reporter friend in Cuba. He was a war reporter who kept a journal on escaped Nazis—those that got away from Germany at the end of the war. In particular, his friend tracked Adolph Eichman, the SS officer who sent millions of Jews to their deaths.

"His friend Ernest Hemingway was at D-Day in June of 1944. Meanwhile, Eichman was in Hungary attempting to capture 750,000

Hungarian Jews and ship them off to concentration camps as part of the Nazi Final Solution."

"Yes, Tom has had us work with Mr. Hemingway, so we know he is always ready to help when it comes to going after Nazis."

"Hemingway was with the French Resistance in Normandy and was able to acquire information on Nazi leaders in Europe who were responsible for the Holocaust. Although he never caught up with Eichman, Hemingway had been told Eichman went home to Austria in May, 1945 to escape prosecution for war crimes. From there it wasn't known where he went. Then, in 1945, former Holocaust prisoner Simon Wiesenthal learned about the serious crimes of Eichman. But there was not enough interest after the war to go after escaped Nazis who were hiding throughout the world. So, the trail for Eichman went cold. Hemingway later reported to Tom that Eichman was living and working in Buenos Aires.

"Tom needs us to go to Argentina and find Eichman. Our work will be investigative only. We will be in a country that sided with Germany during the war and is run by the dictator Juan Peron."

"Are you sure we're up to this, sir?" I asked.

"We have no choice. Simon Wiesenthal believes Eichman can be found now, but he could move and disappear again."

"I hope we can help the cause," Hunter said. "If Simon needs help, I'm willing to do whatever I can. He has helped us on previous takedowns and it is time for us to help him."

"That's true, so true," I said.

We met with Tom as soon as he returned to London. The story he told was sad indeed. Somehow Eichman escaped Germany after the war. It was amazing that there were no published photos of him. He was like a ghost. But one Israeli agent was able to get a photo of

Eichman from a former mistress. Hundreds of copies of the Eichman photo were sent to authorities around the world. Simon, of course, got copies of the photo since he worked for the American Army War Crimes Unit after the war. He was hired by the war crimes investigators because he captured many SS officers himself after the war. Although Simon had information from credible sources that Eichman was in Buenos Aires, the State of Israel was preparing for war with Arab states in 1947. This was the advent of the Jewish state created by a United Nations resolution. And the United States was entering the Cold War with the USSR. As a result, Eichman's escape was unhindered.

"So, what are we to do?" Hunter asked.

"Well, for openers, we will need to follow up on Simon's file on Eichman and the Hemingway notes. We need to go to Argentina to see if we can verify the information on Eichman. Where he lives, works, etc. Is he alive?"

"Tom, we will do whatever is necessary. Just say when," Hunter said.

"Soon."

So, in the spring, 1958, we went to Buenos Aires to follow up on the various leads. The most promising information was recently received from a West German prosecutor who was obsessed with finding Eichman and bringing him to the bar of justice.

Tom prepared a dossier on Eichman for us to read on the BOAC flight to Buenos Aires. We would both study the report and memorize the contents. Then, instructions were to destroy the contents.

The Eichman biographical info was at the beginning. We were aware of what crimes he was responsible for, but the post-war escape information was new evidence. Eichman had been a prisoner of war at the end of the war, but he escaped before he was ever identified as a Nazi leader. He then hid out in the forested areas of Southern Germany. A Black Forest indeed.

For a few years he did work as an itinerant farmhand.

Eventually Eichman connected with the Argentine underground which was all over Europe recruiting ex-Nazis to come to Argentina. Juan Peron of Argentina gave the green light to his secret service to recruit Germans to come to Argentina. Fake passports, safe houses and bribed officials were the order of the day.

Eichman got plugged into that network. He even traveled to Munich to make his connections. Eventually he worked his way down to Italy and got the Red Cross to consider him a refugee so he could travel to Argentina. They gave him a passport and the name Richard Klement.

As he left the Port of Genoa in Italy in the summer of 1950, he no doubt felt he was a free man. No Nuremberg prosecution for him. No more Adolph Eichman. Richard Klement was a new man. He believed he was safe with a new name and a new country. There were reasons to believe he was right.

Argentina welcomed him in 1950. The "underground" got him a job. And it didn't take long for his family to be reunited in his new home country.

Whether he knew it or not, the hunt for Eichman had ended. No country was aggressively tracking this war criminal during most of the 1950's. Although the trail for this Nazi went cold, the families of victims of the Holocaust would never find justice until Eichman was caught and tried for his war crimes.

Our job of finding this Nazi was such that we knew we would never again experience such an enormous responsibility in our lives.

So, of course, we were nervous just thinking about this quest, but we had to keep going forward. Our pretext purpose in travel was to report on travel trends in South America. Argentina was first stop. I was the photojournalist and Hunter the writer for our English-speaking travel journal. The new *WORLD JOURNAL of TRAVEL*. The magazine was based in London and New York. Tom made sure our bona fides were all proper.

Tom reminded us before leaving what Simon said. "Remember, the motto of Shin bet (Israel Intelligence Agency) is Defend and Don't Be Seen."

At the International Airport in Buenos Aires we were met by a cab driver named Enrique who held a sign TRAVEL JOURNAL.

His name was Enrique Cabral and he said the code words "Kentucky Derby" which were on the hat bands of the fedoras we were wearing.

Although Hunter spoke Spanish with Enrique, it became clear that his English was excellent.

"I already brought Father Fitzmaurice to the hotel this morning. I'm sure he will meet you upon arrival. He said he would. And Tom said I should be available for your entire visit. I will always park out back of the hotel. For safety you should know I carry full size Thunder combat pistols, same as Argentine armed forces and law enforcement. My main employment is with Bersa which is a private firearms manu-facturer here in Argentina."

"Tom?"

"Did you say Father Fitzmaurice? Like a priest?" Hunter asked.

"Yes, he is visiting too. Some Irish acquaintance of yours."

Enrique was right. A tall priest was standing outside the Hotel El Escorial and waving his hand as we drove up to the front doors.

"So good to see you all," the priest said.

"I'm Martin Marcelli." (Hunter) I am Felipe Dubroux." (Jordan)

"Very nice to meet you travel journalists," Father Fitzmaurice said.

"Why would an Irish priest be in Argentina?" I asked.

"Frankly, I am on a mission for the Vatican which is rather sensitive. So I need to blend in so that I am not detected, so to speak."

"Like Shin bet," I said.

"Exactly."

Just then Hunter said, "Oh my God. Mr. H. It's you."

"That's right my son, I am a Benedictine priest. As you can probably guess, I was originally a monk. After a few years of solitude in the monastery I came to realize my calling was not to be a monastic monk."

'Yes, I can see that," Hunter said. "It might hinder talking to witnesses and conducting crime investigations."

"As the Pope's emissary I must conduct my investigations."

"So today you are an Irish priest," Hunter said. "Not sure how that helps us in Argentina."

"Well, as a papal emissary in this country I can go anywhere I want. The local government people realize I am an untouchable who is working on special assignment for the Church. They have advised the local bureaucrats that I am going to be with some travel journalists to maintain my work privacy. So, there you go. I am just coming along for the ride."

"Yeah, I don't think you ever go along just for a ride," Hunter said.

"Your man Watson often refers to you as a bloodhound. Is that it? You're really the hound on this mission hunting for Eichman."

"Watson, my dear Watson. He has a way of taking something very confusing and making it easy to understand. Sure, I am a hound. Always and forever. What else could I be?"

"My brother always said you, not Jack Stapleton, were the real Hound of the Baskervilles," Hunter said.

"Funny, that's what Watson always would say. But, you know, in the story the hound was a bloodhound-mastiff cross and he was mistreated by being chained and half starved."

"What about hunting for Eichman? What would a Baskerville hound do?"

"Exactly what we are going to do. Find that demonic little war criminal."

"We know what kind of work he was doing. We have leads on where he might be living. He is now with his wife and three sons. We know their ages," I said.

"And we have the photos. They are from wartime, but they might still help some," Hunter said.

"Boys, we have the element of surprise. He is not expecting us. He knows that he escaped prosecution and with his new country and new identity he has little to worry about. His only fear is Israel and the world knows Israel is immersed in a struggle for its survival."

"Shall we begin?' I asked.

Tom made it clear before we left London that we would need to do top notch work following up on the leads for Eichman in Argentina. Simon Wiesenthal told Tom that if Eichman became aware of our activities that he might disappear forever.

When Enrique drove away from the Hotel El Escorial he told us we were going to visit the family that is believed to have had contact with the Eichmans. We then drove to an area north of the city call Olivos, a seaside residential resort which also was the site of the home of the president of Argentina.

For security reasons we were not told the last name of the family that we were meeting.

"Hello, come in, you must be here for father," the young lady said. "I am Sylvia and hope to talk to you gentlemen in a bit."

"I am Lothar. It is nice to meet you. You must be Father Fitzmaurice and these are the journalists. Which one is Marcelli?"

"That's me sir," Hunter said. "Are you related to the famous Marcelli equestrian family in Buenos Aires?"

"No, but I certainly know the Marcelli's are some of the best riders in Argentina and therefore the best in the world."

It was amazing when Lothar reached out to shake hands, his hand placement was perfect. We had been told he was blind.

"My honor, Lothar," Father Fitzmaurice said.

"I can feel you are a man of many talents, Father."

"And I feel you are a man who has suffered at the hands of some very bad people."

"I guess they were people, but they were depraved and their actions were unpardonable, Father."

"I understand, Lothar. You were at Dachau."

"It was bad for me but I'm still alive. So many died. I saw the horror before they destroyed my eyesight. They can't erase my memory. I am a lawyer by profession and I was taught to remember details and facts and I do."

"What about Eichman?" I asked. "I am Felipe Dubroux."

"Hello Felipe. The secret intelligence people have talked to me and they don't understand how a blind man could identify this war criminal Eichman. Some of us will never forget. That's the thing. That's the difference. I want this man brought to justice and until then I will not rest. It's that simple."

"I appreciate your words and your commitment. We have the same goal, Lothar," Father Fitzmaurice said.

"Sylvia, please come sit down. Please tell our friends what you learned about Eichman."

Of course, she did what her father asked. She told us about meeting "Nick" Eichman at a school event. When he visited at her home he expressed his opinions in favor of Nazi Germany. He said his father was in the Third Reich. He did not know Sylvia was Jewish since she was being raised Christian. The Eichman boy's comments scared this persecuted family into conducting their own investigation into the Eichmans.

"Sylvia, you are the bravest young lady I have ever met," Father said. "You and your father traveled a great distance to track down the Eichman clan. And you actually entered their home?"

She said she asked to meet Nick's family. He got angry at Sylvia, but she persisted and saw the man in the photos. It was him. He talked to her. He knew they were teenagers and Nick was a boyfriend. The family said he was the uncle, but the word "father" slipped out. Sylvia knew then that they were hiding him and they had a different name for him.

"You mean Ricardo Klement?" I asked.

"That's it. Klement the uncle is really Eichman the father. Besides the photo, we had descriptions of his speech and mannerisms. It all matched," Lothar said.

"So we know this is Eichman. We need you to convince the Israelis to seize the time and capture this war criminal. If not, we were told by our friend, Attorney General Fritz Bayer in Germany, that he will go after Eichman and try to extradite."

"We will advise the powers in Israel that this may be the only chance they have left to get him, "Father said. "If Germany comes after him he may go into hiding, never to be found."

"Yes, you are right," Lothar said. "The Nazi network here will hide him again."

"The Prime Minister David Ben-Gurion needs to know that catching and prosecuting Eichman is very very important to the world. These crimes cannot be forgotten or they will happen again. Do you understand?"

"It has become even more important now and we understand," Father said.

"You need to go check this business out for yourself. Maybe it's the only hope for Simon Wiescnthal to get the support he needs. None of us can afford to do what needs to be done. If Israel won't pursue this war criminal then West Germany will. Although the German Attorney General is sincere, I can't help but think Eichman will get word of any attempt to arrest him in Argentina. The State of Israel must do this."

"We do understand, Lothar," Father Fitzmaurice said.

The next move was to collect Lothar's surveillance information. Where was Eichman, where did he work? When did he travel daily? Who else could we trust to get information on this war criminal?

Then it was time to activate our plan with Enrique, our armed chauffer and Papal Emissary Father Fitzmaurice (Sherlock Holmes).

It was clear we needed to follow the plan which Lothar assisted with. Hunter and I felt like we were just along for the ride. Enrique and Father Fitzmaurice were in the know. We asked about the plan but they just said be patient. "We don't know yet." But they did know. We were going to Eichman's house on Chacabuco Street. Exactly where Sylvia went when she met Mr. Evil.

Chacabuco Street

"Get that fancy camera ready to shoot," Enrique yelled at me. "We're getting close."

"Maybe I better take the camera, "Hunter said." I can speak Spanish and German if we need to talk to one of the neighbors or Eichman himself."

"Good thinking. I would just stutter in English if I get confronted. If I met Eichman I might try to tackle him and hold him down until Hunter comes and helps me finish him off."

"Jordo, we can't do that."

"I know, I know."

"Sure, give him the camera. I have the guns. Father has the rosary."

"I guess I've got nothing."

"Jordan, you're my wingman. You've got the brains. Keep thinking because if this scheme goes south you need to think quick."

"Hand me that halter and lead rope under the front seat please," Hunter said. "I'm looking for two horses that got loose about a mile away. They belong to Mr. Marcelli from the Argentine Olympic team."

Hunter got out of the car and proceeded down Chacabuco Street and walked right in front of the house Sylvia and Lothar told us about at 4261 Chacabuco. There were children kicking a ball in the yard. Hunter spoke with them. He held the halter and lead rope up above his head. Enrique snapped some shots using a long-range lens on the camera he had around his neck. We were parked a few hundred yards away from the house and near some trees and brush cover.

Then it happened. A man came into the front yard after coming around the side of the nondescript impoverished looking residence. He approached Hunter who again held the horse tack high above his head.

"Perfect. That's good," Enrique said as he took more pictures which later would show pretty clearly the man was Adolph Eichman.

Hunter frantically pointed his hands in multiple directions. Then Eichman did the same. Soon the children in the front yard were pointing their hands in all directions.

Then Hunter took off running away from the area as if he was in search of the horses.

We did not see Hunter again until a few hours later. He was a mess and covered with dried blood, his own.

"What happened brother," I asked.

"Long story. Doesn't matter. I saw him. I talked to him. I took his picture when he looked up at the halter."

"If you're trying to catch two horses why do you only have one halter and rope?" Eichman asked me.

I told him the horses were brother and sister and if you catch one then the other will come along.

"Yes, of course," he said.

"What made you think about the horse tack?" Holmes asked.

"In Simon's brief there was mention of horse carts in the neighborhood. People got their fresh daily bread delivered by horse cart."

"That was an excellent plan, Hunter," Holmes said.

"Thank you, sir."

"I was able to get my long-range shots, but if you shot up close photos they will be very helpful," Enrique said. "I can develop the film at my office. We have a dark room for the advertising department."

"As for the blood, I had to cross over some barbed wire fences which were not in the best shape. I tripped on one and ended up cutting my back and legs. Thank God I had a tetanus shot before we left London. Thanks to Jordan."

"Anytime buddy."

"The whole thing was weird. Eichman spoke German. I spoke Spanish. I knew what he was saying but I thought I should stick to Spanish since I worked for the Marcellis."

"Who are the Marcellis?" he asked." I said they're like Hans Günter Winkler of Germany. He understood I must be important if I worked for Argentines who were as successful as Winkler."

"Winkler and Halla," he said. "I agreed. He knew Winkler's great show jumper mare was named Halla. That's when I said I had to go and I took off running away from his house. The boys said they had seen horses run through the back lot area. So that's where I went, and I just kept going. I ran like hell. I was so scared and felt like this guy might try to execute me. It was like the dream you have as a kid when you're being chased by the bad guys and when you yell for help your voice doesn't work. I had looked Evil and Death in the eye and it was terrifying. I could feel murder. It was horrible, but I just followed the plan and tried to keep breathing."

"Thank God it was you, Hunter," I said. "I would have tried to throw a brick at him and he might have killed me."

"Jordo, you know I would save you. No matter what, brother."

"It's over now boys, I think."

"Simon will be relieved to know we have had success in identifying Eichman," Holmes said.

"Excellent work," Enrique said.

We thought we should return to visit Lothar and Sylvia. However, Enrique said he would meet with them in a quiet manner so no attention would be called to their family. Enrique believed Lothar and Sylvia were at risk of Nazi retaliation if anyone learned about their involvement. Further, he said Lothar was thinking about sending Sylvia to the United States for school and personal safety.

On the way back to El Escorial, Enrique asked us if we had any special requests before leaving Buenos Aires.

"Absolutely," Hunter said. "Jordan and I are Kentucky boys and we need to ride some horses before we leave this beautiful city."

"So, you probably want to go to Palermo district where they have all the riding clubs," Enrique said.

"Indeed we do. We would like to visit the Marcelli Stables."

"It used to be the Don Santiago racing barn providing stalls for the horses racing at the Palermo track. They'll have horses and saddles. We can get you boots there too. Then go for a ride at Los Bosques de Palermo—the forested parks of Buenos Aires," Enrique said.

"We can arrange that," Mr. Holmes said. "I'm very proud of you boys. It is so important to remember your heritage. I must go to your State of Kentucky someday. It has always been a dream of mine to visit the bluegrass fiefdom."

"Absolutely."

We went with Enrique straightaway to Marcelli Stables in the Palermo neighborhood of Buenos Aires and were surprised to learn it was Estancia Day (gaucho dress) in Buenos Aires. Hunter loved his gaucho hat and outfit and threatened to stay in Argentina forever. I had not seen him so happy since he scored a touchdown in eighth grade on a punt return in a football game.

"Jordo, I don't think I can ever leave Los Bosques, the Forests. I love this place. I want to live here, work here and even die here. It is so otherworldly. So beautiful. And I want to be a gaucho, even if it's just a part-time job. I am a gaucho, damn it. You know I am."

"You are a gaucho, Hunter. For sure. Maybe when we finish our work with Nazis we can come back and both of us can be gauchos," I said.

"But I'm afraid we'll never finish with the Nazi work. Not in this lifetime. I may have to wait for my next life to be a gaucho," Hunter sighed.

"I'll bring you back. I promise. Next year we will go to the Pampas and live with real gauchos."

"Thanks Jordo, you're the best, man."

CHAPTER 7

HEMINGWAY'S REVENGE

"I AM SO GLAD YOU boys made it back and were successful," Tom said. We met with him at El Duque the day after we got back. "Plan on staying here for a few days before you go to Italy."

"Italy?" Hunter said. "I've always wanted to go to Italy, but what for?"

"You remember the file on Eichman had reference to the fake passport and fake name. Well, our team has obtained a copy of his original passport which was issued by the Red Cross in Genoa, Italy."

"Are we going after the Red Cross?" I asked.

"Well, yes."

Then the explaining took place. Tom was right. We were going to Italy and going after the Red Cross.

It turns out that Enrique got access to the Eichman/Klement passport and had Holmes deliver a copy to Tom.

We knew Enrique Cabral was a man of many talents, but we really didn't know who or what he really was. Hunter and I did conclude he would probably figure into our future. He was just so damn good at everything. Exactly what we needed. Always.

As for Italy, it was a simple mission. Get that Nazi out of the Red Cross. If possible get the list of Nazis he has sent around the world.

And we would do everything possible to track down Horst Fuldner in Genoa or wherever he was in Italy. He was part of the scheme to get Nazis to Argentina.

"How could the Red Cross be part of this scheme?"

Holmes told Tom that his limited experience with crime in Italy suggested our Italian mission would be a job fraught with danger. Holmes had prior experience with a Neapolitan criminal brotherhood known as the Red Circle. "Once a member, always a member." There was no getting out of a crime family. Very much like the Black Hand, *La Mano Nera* which had extortion and protection rackets.

"Tom, maybe your friend in Cuba can help," Hunter said. "He was in the Red Cross in Italy in World War I."

"That's exactly what Holmes thought, so he paid a visit to Cuba after leaving Argentina. He said Hemingway had heard about the Nazi infiltration into the Red Cross and personally felt a moral obligation to help however he could."

"I thought it was great that Holmes told you boys he would go to Kentucky," Tom said.

"I didn't know if he really meant it," I said.

"Maybe he did. It doesn't really matter. It's the point of it all. He respects our love of the horse. I think some people are jealous of what we have in Kentucky. The great horses. The Derby. And bourbon."

"Your right, Hunter, it really made an impression when he learned we wanted to ride in Los Bosques. I guess we better keep in mind what he said. Remember our heritage."

"We do and we will, Jordan. I can make that promise. But we have to get ready for this next business, Genoa. Our visit to the village of Christopher Columbus. And after this business is over we will go to Rome for the ride of a lifetime. We will ride the Tuscan hills on horseback."

"That sounds great. I'll do it," I said.

"Where will we meet Hemingway, Hunter?"

"Tom made it sound like he would find us in Genoa. Maybe he's already there doing some legwork.

"Jordan, don't you think Hemingway might be too busy to just pick up and come to Europe, leaving his wife and writing life behind in Cuba?"

"I don't know. He came to London when Tom needed his help with the judges who were being pressured by the Nazi law professors."

We met up with Mr. Hemingway in Rome. He told us he had been to the American Red Cross office in Naples to see if he could learn anything about a Nazi mole in the Italian Red Cross. What he learned was very disturbing. Mussolini himself placed operatives in the Red Cross during his time in power as leader of the Fascist Party and Prime Minister of Italy from 1922 to 1943.

"We know Mussolini had total control of Italy with his secret police in the 1920's and his tactics became the model for dictators like Hitler and Franco," Hemingway said.

"It only stands to reason that he placed his people in the Red Cross for control and adherence to nationalistic goals, especially with regard to refugees. Then at the end of the war they were able to use the Passport Refugee division for their own purposes. Funny thing, it wasn't really political. It was more like a protection racket and it was all about money. Pay the price and be a refugee. The old guard from

Mussolini ran this scam for years after the war. We are going to put an end to it," Hemingway promised.

"I was able to find some information on Horst Fuldner. He is one of the Nazis in Argentina who headed up the network to get Germans to South America. Argentina wanted and still wants engineers, scientists, doctors and military men. It doesn't matter that they are Nazis. All the better according to Horst."

"What about Genoa? Who is in charge of that office and what do we do?" Hunter asked.

"Believe it or not Mussolini's nephew is who we are looking for. Don Angelino (Mussolini). He doesn't use his last name. Never did since Uncle Benito put him in the Red Cross to keep an eye on the organization. Don Angelino was always said to be a little slow on the uptake."

"But he has probably made a lot of money, despite being the dictator's idiot nephew." I said.

"He is a wealthy man indeed," Hemingway said. "And that is the problem. What do we do with this guy? Tom said we still have friends from Resistance days who could easily turn Don Angelino's small mansion into smithereens and dust."

"What are the alternatives?" Hunter asked.

"I think we need to take an idea from the playbook of the Great Ones who showed us how to handle the thieves in Puerto Rico and California," I said.

"You mean give 'em a way out?"

"Exactly."

"What do you propose, Jordan?" Hemingway asked.

"Well, when we started this quest we decided we were not ever going to be vigilantes or killers. We are about justice, but in this case I think we have to actually scare the hell out of the Mussolini nephew."

"I agree," Hemingway said.

"You're pretty quick on the trigger, sir, aren't you?" Hunter said.

"Maybe, son. Yeah, maybe. I got pretty deep into all the war years. Maybe too much so. I probably shouldn't be making these kind of decisions, boys. Thanks for calling me out, Hunter."

"I didn't mean it like that. It's just that we told Sister Ansilio we would do justice, not kill."

"That's legit, Hunter."

"But we need to let him believe he faces dire consequences if he doesn't turn over his list of refugee Nazis like Eichman," I said.

"You mean like what happened in New Jersey with the Von Stempler brothers?" Hunter asked.

"Mr. Bruno had the Nazis look out the window so they could see their car blow up. That got 'em going."

"We can blow up his mansion on the hill," Hemingway suggested. "We have the manpower. Tom gave me the info we need to reach out for help to get that job done."

"Really?" Hunter asked.

"Hunter, look, we need that list. And he won't give it up unless we put big pressure on. Words alone won't do," I said.

So the trap was set. We approached Don Angelino telling him we needed a passport to South America and we would pay big money. We had an uncle who was in the SS and the authorities had recently uncovered evidence of his involvement in a genocidal attack in Latvia. In addition, he was suspected of having a treasure trove of stolen art.

Our uncle was a successful businessman and he would pay top dollar for help. He could afford it. We were South Africans.

Don Angelino was all about it. This was a big job. Like the big money times after the war.

We agreed to meet the next day for lunch at uncle's hotel in downtown Genoa. We picked the Albergo Caffaro Hotel because of the great view of the city and because it was close to city centre. For some reason, Hunter always demanded being near city centre whenever we went to a new town or city. I think he always wanted to walk through a town to get a feel for it. It is what we did as kids. We would go to downtown Louisville and walk around. Hunter always wanted to go to the places that were not the high-class areas. He very much enjoyed seeing the panhandlers, pickpockets and shoeshine boys. We would always talk to the street people. Hunter would ask them simple questions and then he always seemed amazed at what they said. How they told their story is what he called it.

Anyway, Don Angelino showed up as planned.

"He thinks he's going to cut a fat hog, Jordo. My God is he going to be shocked," Hunter said.

We began talks in earnest and then it happened.

"Hey boys, look over on the hill out the big window. That's my house."

"Here's the deal Mr. Mussolini," Hunter said. "I need the list of all Nazis you have provided with fake passports. We need the names, dates and location of these so-called refugees. And don't lie damnit. We already know about your involvement with Ricardo Klement."

"What about Mr. Klement?"

"There is no Klement," I said. "He's Eichman."

"I do not have your answer to my request for this list. I have no alternative then," Hunter said. He then walked to the large window with the walkout balcony. He waived a green flag several times over his head.

"What is he doing?" Don Angelino Mussolini asked.

"He is giving our people the green light to blow up your mansion. Any people in your home are being escorted out right now. In one minute your mansion on the hill will be a pile of rubble. We want that list. We want it now."

Then the explosion happened and Mussolini fell to his knees just like the Nazi ravenmaster did in Moscow. He muttered Italian phrases of anger with some curses at the deity for allowing this to happen.

"Just like Il Duce at the end, you have fallen to your knees. His life was over. You still have a chance to continue breathing but you must get us that list of Nazis who you ran through the Red Cross as refugees.

"Likewise, you have one more minute to decide, I said." "We cannot and will not wait."

Don Angelino was hysterical but he did not want to die.

"I can't die. I can't do it. Not for these Nazi bastards. I hate all of them. They're no good rotten sons of bitches. I just do it for the money. I won't die for them. I won't. You can have all my records so take them all. I quit the Red Cross. I will not die for the Nazis. They never liked us Italians. And I never like them. None of them."

At that moment there was a knock on the door and then it opened. It was Shev Parlitzkin from Mossad.

"I'm here for the list," he said.

"We can have all the files," Hunter said. "The Red Cross man states he will not die for the Nazis. He just did it for the money."

"We will deal with that issue on another day. I have secure transportation outside. We need to leave right away. Mr. Mussolini will come with us."

"Of course," I said.

"He's all yours," Hunter added.

They were going to leave for Israel with the files. There they would meet with Tuviah Friedman at Yad Vashem at the Holocaust Memorial Center. That was all we knew. That was all we needed to know. Like Holmes told us, do your job right and let the authorities handle the final arrest and prosecution.

We left Genoa and returned to Rome. As promised, Hunter made arrangements to go riding with a local equestrian family. When we arrived I realized he had contacted the Marcelli family in Rome. (They were relatives of the famous Marcelli family in Argentina). We then went by bus on a short trip to Tuscany to ride in an area known as Montepulciano.

The Tuscan hills were magnificent as one would expect. We were surrounded by vineyards and olive groves. Although the ride was peaceful and beautiful, it was hard to erase the picture emblazoned on our brains of the Mussolini mansion on the hill in Genoa blowing up.

By the end of the afternoon, we were no longer thinking about the Mussolini mansion. We stopped at a vineyard for the winetasting of several wines, including the famous *Nobile de Montepulciano*. We were also provided local specialty foods.

I thanked Hunter for his taking serious what Holmes said about respecting our Kentucky heritage. Holmes was right. We honored our families and ourselves. *Never forget* is what we believed. *It must be how we live, I thought.*

"Hunter, next year or as soon as possible, we will go back to Argentina, and I promise we will go stay on an estancia (ranch) in the Pampas. This day in Tuscany has made me realize how lucky we are to be from Kentucky, the land of the noble beast, the horse."

By the time we got back to London the Nazi list of Mussolini's nephew had been reviewed by Tom and Sherlock Holmes. The information provided in the list supported restarting a lot of investigations that had gone dormant for lack of necessary leads. The list had a considerable amount of up-to-date info on many ex-Nazis who were still paying off private debts to Mussolini and his gang. And a gang it was. Don Angelino had set up a criminal collection agency that did not need to use force for collection, just extortion. Threats of disclosure, mainly. It worked. The Nazis kept paying because they were afraid of being discovered. The result was Tom had more intelligence on Nazi crimes and Nazi whereabouts.

"You will find this hard to believe. I did. But we have evidence of a Nazi network in the proposed fiftieth state, Hawaii."

"Tom, we have never even heard of any Nazis in Hawaii," I said.

"It does make some sense. The last place you'd expect," Hunter said.

"Well, they are there in every city in the islands. They have a Nazi controlled financial empire the likes of which we have never seen anywhere.

"The challenge will be devising a plan to topple or destroy this enterprise. I have asked Mr. Holmes and Dr. Watson to help us with this mission."

CHAPTER 8

KNOCKING ON SAXON'S DOOR

THE DECISION WAS MADE FOR us as to where to go in Hawaii which was good since neither of us had any knowledge about or experience in Hawaii. We would start off in the city of Honolulu which is on the island of Oahu. There's a total of eight volcanic islands that are called the Hawaiian Islands. The plan was to visit all islands necessary to get the plan set for the attack on Saxony Bank of Hawaii.

"What is Saxony? Hunter asked. "It doesn't exactly fit in Hawaii."

"You're right," Tom said.

"It is one of the German states and the capital is Dresden."

"Why call it Saxony Bank? Is it because of what happened there during the war?" Hunter asked. "The bombing of Dresden?"

"Maybe. We know Dresden was not a war production city. It was known for its architecture and the arts."

I told Tom we knew an army man who was in Dresden during the bombing in February, 1945. He was an acquaintance of Hunter's. "His name is Kurt Vonnegut."

"Maybe you boys should meet up with your friend Vonnegut. Where is he?"

"Right now, he is here in London studying playwriting. He is a storyteller who is here trying to decide if he should write plays, novels or something else."

So, we arranged the meet.

"Hunter, how can I help you?" Mr. Vonnegut asked.

"I'm wondering about Dresden."

"I've been wondering about Dresden since I left Germany in the spring 1945. It has gotten the better of me on several days and nights since the bombing. It was horrific and it never should have happened. It was not a war target. It became a people target. God-awful. There are days... I don't know. Dresden tears me apart. Twenty-five thousand or more people died. I was lucky to live through the bombing. As you know, I was a prisoner of war being held in a makeshift prison."

"Why were you a prisoner?" Hunter asked.

"I got caught by the enemy."

"Not a good question, Kurt. I mean what happened. How did you become a POW?"

"At the Battle of the Bulge, we were outmanned and outgunned. So, the 106th Infantry Division gave up almost 6,000 American soldiers around Christmas, 1944. We were surrounded and cut off from our army and supplies. You remember that's when they called in General Patton."

"The Army brass didn't care for Patton until they got into trouble. Then they begged him to come to the rescue."

"That's right, Hunter. But that was too late for some of us with the 106th Infantry.

"Churchill said the Battle of the Bulge was the greatest American battle of the war.

"Maybe it was, but we weren't ready for the last big drive of the German Army with their 200,000 men and 1,000 tanks. When they broke through our front we were surrounded. Somehow I lived through the battle at the Ardennes Forest only to end up in Dresden for the bombing."

"Well, Mr. Vonnegut, what can you tell us about Saxony. Why would Nazis name a bank after Saxony?" I asked.

"Of course, Dresden is the capital of Saxony. Many German people believe the Allies were cruel in the bombing campaign. It has even been used as a rallying cry for Neo-Nazis and right-wing extremists in Germany since the war."

"Really?"

"Don't think it all couldn't happen again. The Nazis convinced the German people what they were doing was the right thing. They could come back if we let our guard down."

"Is there a connection between the Nazis who moved major ill-gotten funds into Saxony Bank of Hawaii and Dresden?" I asked.

"Why else call it Saxony? Yes, I'm sure of it. They will use Dresden as a rallying cry. You'll see. If you meet with the bankers, they will no doubt tell you the same story about restoring art and architecture to Dresden. But Nazis are devious bastards. I think they're using Dresden for a return to power."

"Oh my God."

"I think you are right, Kurt. Thanks for your help. We will meet again when it is safe after our work is done with Saxony Bank of Hawaii."

"So it goes my friends. Be safe, Hunter and Jordan."

"Yes, Kurt, thank you for your insight. I don't think we fully understood what Dresden meant to the German people," I said.

"And so it goes and so it goes."

When we returned to meet with Tom after the Vonnegut debriefing both Holmes and Watson were in attendance.

"My guess is your friend Vonnegut connected the dots."

"That's right, Tom"

"I thought you should hear about Dresden from someone who was there. There is no other way to truly understand."

"Well, we understand now why they call it Saxony Bank of Hawaii."

"That's right. It's part of the plan to appeal to sympathies. It works. Everyone feels bad about what happened to Dresden."

"So, what should we do, Tom?"

"You should make contact with Baron Adalbert Gruner and Max Heidegger."

"Who are they?" Hunter asked.

"They are us," Holmes exclaimed as he and Watson stood up and bowed. "We are ex-Nazi sympathizers who will spearhead the efforts to use Dresden to help Saxony Bank get into Europe in an effort to reestablish the financial foundation for the emergence of the new Reich. There are already major efforts going on in Germany for a Neo-Nazi movement. We saw this during the Eichman mission. Israel and Germany are now both concerned that 1959 could bring back a serious Nazi movement in Germany. And Saxony Bank of Hawaii wants to be part of this effort."

"This is a big deal," I said.

"We hope to make it a nothing deal," Tom said.

"Sounds like Jordan and I are going to have company in Hawaii."

"That's right, Hunter. You will be traveling with Baron Gruner and his attaché. The Baron is from Austria and was sympathetic to the Reich."

"This is going to be interesting," Hunter surmised.

"*Jawohl, mein Kommandant,*" the Baron said.

When we arrived in Hawaii, we were taken to the Navy Housing Office at Pearl Harbor and advised by our military escort that since we were there on a mission which required security clearances, we would be provided quarters for command officers.

"I had no idea our military stayed in such nice places," Jordan said.

"They don't, Jordo. These are general quarters—for the brass only. The whole time I was in the Air Force I was never in a place this nice."

We were instructed to make the arrangements to meet with the international bankers at Saxony Bank.

That was a good strategy even though the bank didn't have an international department. They took the bait and wanted to meet with the international art brokers from Switzerland.

At the first meeting with the Saxons, Hunter and I did our usual and customary Boudreaux dog-and-pony show for the German bankers in Hawaii. As a result, a meeting was set up for Baron Albert Gruner and attaché Max Heidegger.

"There must be some backstory to the names," Hunter said to Watson.

"That is for sure. You are a perceptive young man, Hunter. Mr. Max Heidegger was a German schoolmaster at the Priory School in a village on the moors in the North of England. He died trying to save a student. Very noble. From the Holmes short story '*The Adventure of the Priory School*.'"

"My character is not such a nice guy. He was a notorious aristocrat from Austria. And he is the perfect man for this job with Bank of Saxony. He was in *The Adventure of the Illustrious Client*."

"That is the Baron. A bad actor you would say. I'm sure he is not remembered by anyone except the enthusiasts of the Holmes' canon. But it should be noted that Baron Albert Gruner was said to have been the most dangerous man in Europe. I intend to achieve that level of demonic excellence in this mission."

Our plan was simple. We explain to the Nazi bankers that they need to make an investment in the movement that has already started. The resurgence of the Reich.

"Watson, you are an attaché to what?" I asked.

"It's not clear. Possibly a future state. That may depend on the commitment of these stingy bankers."

"If they are truly the Nazis we think they are, then there won't be a problem. They will shower us with money because we are the only game there is."

"I think you're right, Baron," Hunter said. "They have been waiting for this day since April 30, 1945, the day their Fuhrer committed suicide by gunshot after taking a cyanide capsule."

"He didn't trust the cyanide?" Watson queried.

"No, Max Heidegger. He was raving mad and paranoid at the end. He trusted nothing and nobody."

"The Baron is right," Hunter said. "Hitler was on drugs like methamphetamines and barbiturates.

"He was a very confused dictator. Everyone agrees he was nutso at the end," Hunter said.

"Even before, he was pretty wacked out," I said. "He thought he knew more than his generals. He made many mistakes overruling the German military's strategies and tactics."

"Good for us. Bad for them."

"And now the Saxons believe they have the opportunity to bring back the Hitler style of leadership. We will promise them another hero. That's what they want. A fearless leader who will tell them what they want to hear. And he will be an Aryan man who believes in the divinity of his race."

At the Saxony Bank

As we entered the large boardroom at Saxony Bank in Oahu, we were reminded of our takedown of the Puerto Rican Nazis in New York at Chase Manhattan Bank.

"Come right in Baron Gruner," the confident bank executive barked out. "I am Horst Bruner. We're Gruner and Bruner."

There was a polite chuckle and we felt a sense of confidence this meeting would work out.

"And this is your attaché, Max Heidegger."

"*Jawohl, mein Kommandant,*" Max exclaimed in a voice louder than Bruner's.

"The Boudreaux team made it clear that serious plans are afoot back home to bring back the Reich."

"That is exactly right," Baron Gruner said. "All that is needed is a financial commitment equal to the task."

"You mean to have the support of Saxony Bank?"

"That is correct," the Baron said.

"It comes down to this, gentlemen. If you support our movement then you have the opportunity to get involved at this early stage. Your support and contributions will have a significant impact."

The Baron Gruner then advised the bankers that we were working with the BND (Federal Intelligence Service) out of Berlin and most of our contacts were former SS and Gestapo, recruited to be part of the Gehlen Organization (the Org) which was the predecessor to BND.

The truth was the "Org" had over 100 former SS and Gestapo officers. One of those officers was Alois Brunner, Eichman's deputy.

"Well, men, this is the day we have been waiting for. A chance to return to power. We have the capital. We only need the will of the people."

"And now we have it," Baron Gruner said.

"If you have the cooperation of the BND, then we are with you. We will provide the funding that is needed to bring back our way of life," Saxony Bank President Horst Bruner said.

"We have decided to hold our first rally in Berlin," Baron said. "Then we will go to all the major cities. We will invite many speakers to show the unity of the German people. We will rebuild the party gradually just like in 1933 in Nuremberg and later rallies. The police in Berlin will support us just as they did in Nuremberg. We will build with a Rally for Victory and then a Rally for Unity and Strength. Eventually we will have a Rally for Power and finally a Rally for the Will."

"Just like before," Bruner said. "Maybe Riefenstahl will give us another film and we can create a new version of the Cathedral of Light."

"Yes, you see the vision, Herr Bruner. We can do all of this if we have the funds."

"The Bank of Saxony is at your command, Baron. It has always been our plan to return to Germany and recapture our land."

"We have significant reserves in Switzerland than can be made readily available for our plans. We will also have private banking operations in Switzerland with a goal of moving into Germany. Hawaii has provided us protection and anonymity. We are now ready to rejoin our people with the financial resources that will support the future."

"How did your bank grow to be so successful in Hawaii?"

"That's easy. We started with a lot of gold and valuable works of art. Germany was good to us and now it is time to repay the debt. Our assets exceed five billion Deutsche Marks. We are ready to compete with rival Deutsche Bank which was started in 1870 by the King of Prussia."

"Shall we celebrate this new partnership? We will bring unity back to our people."

It was all planned out with the return to Germany by the principals of the bank. The ultimate goal was to reclaim Dresden which meant that reunification of Germany would be part of the plan going forward.

Finally, we left Hawaii with enough details on the bank's financial plans to restore the Reich to Germany that the Federal Intelligence Service (BND) would be able to successfully go after the bank and prosecute the principals. Switzerland would agree to work with Germany on freezing the assets of this Nazi financial organization.

We hoped our efforts would help prevent the rise of a new Reich. So we said goodbye to Hawaii, but we were convinced it would not be long before we would be tracking down Nazis somewhere else in the world.

ABOUT THE AUTHOR

The author J. Michael Moriarty never knew or met Hunter Thompson. Moriarty was learning how to become a reporter while HST was crashing the boards at the *Rolling Stone* with *Fear and Loathing*.

He went to law school after journalism school, hoping to become an investigative reporter. That didn't happen, so Moriarty started practicing law in his hometown of Omaha, Nebraska.

Recently, Moriarty has redirected his efforts to writing again. First came the Hemingway stories (*Hemingway's Retreat* and *Hemingway's Return to England*).

Now he is bringing back another legend from journalism and the culture wars.

Doctor Gonzo. Hunter Thompson. The author hopes to write a series of books on Hunter Thompson as a young Nazi hunter. The first book is *The Return of Hunter S. Thompson, An Untold Story of Nazi Hunting*.

Moriarty believes Thompson would have been a steadfast Nazi hunter if he had the opportunity to pursue that vocation. The author gives him that chance.

ABOUT THE EDITOR

Tom Moriarty is the editor and virtual co-author of the Hunter Thompson series known as the *Return of Hunter S. Thompson*.

Tom was the idea guy behind the stories told by his younger brother.

Although Tom has left us, the ideas and inspiration continue on. He just knew.

"We have seen this movie before my friends. The Nazis have escaped Justice. Our job is to find them and take Justice to them."